Meet the team:

Alex – A quiet lad from Northumbria, Alex leads the team in survival skills. His dad is in the SAS and Alex is determined to follow in his footsteps, whatever it takes. He who dares . . .

Li – Expert in martial arts and free-climbing, Li can get to grips with most situations . . .

Paulo – The laid-back Argentinian is a mechanical genius, and with his medical skills he can patch up injuries as well as motors . . .

Hex – An ace hacker, Hex is first rate at code-breaking and can bypass most security systems . . .

Amber – Her top navigational skills mean the team are rarely lost. Rarely lost for words either, rich-girl Amber can show some serious attitude . . .

With plenty of hard work and training, together they are Alpha Force – an elite squad of young people dedicated to combating injustice throughout the world.

In *Hunted* Alpha Force go head to head with a ruthless gang of ivory poachers in Zambia.

www.kidsat_____rce

D0414070

CHRIS RYAN

ALPHA FORCE

HUNTED

RED
FOX

ALPHA FORCE: HUNTED
A RED FOX BOOK : 9780099464259

First published in Great Britain by Red Fox,
an imprint of Random House Children's Books

This edition published 2004

7 9 10 8 6

The Random House Group Limited supports The Forest Stewardship
Council (FSC), the leading international forest certification organisation.
All our titles that are printed on Greenpeace approved FSC certified paper
carry the FSC logo. Our paper procurement policy can be found at:
www.rbooks.co.uk/environment

Typeset in Sabon by Palimpsest Book Production Limited,
Polmont, Stirlingshire

Red Fox Books are published by Random House Children's Books,
61–63 Uxbridge Road, London W5 5SA,
a division of The Random House Group Ltd

Addresses for companies within The Random House Group Limited
can be found at:
www.randomhouse.co.uk/offices.htm

THE RANDOM HOUSE GROUP Limited Reg. No. 954009
www.kidsatrandomhouse.co.uk

A CIP catalogue record for this book is available from the British Library.

Printed and bound in Great Britain by
CPI Cox & Wyman, Reading, RG1 8EX

ALPHA FORCE

The field of
operation...

DEM. REP.
CONGO   TANZANIA

ANGOLA   MALAWI
ZAMBIA
MOZAMBIQUE
ZIMBABWE
NAMIBIA
BOTSWANA

SOUTH
AFRICA

PROLOGUE
THE DEAL

Families of elephants lifted their trunks, sniffing the air. In a rush of wind and thunder, the white belly of the plane roared overhead. The craft was flying at low altitude, looking for the landing strip. It sent buffalo pouring into the river. Herds of antelope, zebra and springbok scattered, startled, across the plains.

The plane skimmed the tops of the trees, beginning its final descent. The moment the wheels grazed the ground, the pilot stamped on the brakes. Dust rose up in hot ochre clouds.

The plane slowed to a halt just short of where the poachers waited with their battered Land Rover. There were three of them in combat fatigues, ammunition belts crossed over their shoulders. One had a scar in the brown skin of his cheek. The other two were white – one wore a hyena tooth set in silver on a chain around his neck; the other had a dirty yellow bandanna tied around his forehead.

They heard a noise among the trees and automatically levelled their weapons. A brown hyena trotted out of the bush, long fur topped by a tawny mane on its powerful shoulders. Its jaws were clamped around the bloody, torn-off leg of a wildebeest. The poachers lowered their weapons. They didn't expect any trouble in this remote part of the Zambian bush, but they weren't taking any chances. And you never knew – something might appear that was worth shooting.

The plane door opened. A slight figure got out and walked towards them. He had delicate oriental features; wisps of grey punctuated the jet-black hair. His lightweight, sand-coloured suit showed little creasing, despite the heat and the long journey he had made.

The poacher with the yellow bandanna reached behind into the Land Rover and pulled out a dusty sack. It was heavy. He needed both hands to lift it.

The oriental man put a hand out towards the sack. The diamonds on his Gucci watch glinted in the setting sun. He touched the bulging underside of the sack, feeling the shape of the contents. It wouldn't be the first time a poacher had tried to give him a live snake to take home instead of the goods he had paid for. His eyes betrayed no emotion.

'Show me,' he said.

The poacher kneeled down and tipped out the contents of the sack. Chunks of ivory tumbled onto the golden earth – giant hollow tusks sawn into pieces. Some of them were wide like sections of drainpipe, some were small like napkin rings. Many of the bigger pieces had bloody flesh clinging to them where they had been hacked out of the faces of elephants.

The buyer nodded and smiled. His face creased around his eyes like old tissue paper. While the poacher with the bandanna scooped up the ivory pieces and put them back in the sack, the other two fetched more from the jeep.

The buyer walked the short distance to the plane and came back with an envelope. He held it out. The poacher with the scar took it and counted it. Two thousand American dollars. He nodded to his companions.

The oriental man picked up the three sacks of ivory. Although they were heavy he carried them easily and loaded them into his plane. Then he turned to the poachers and said, 'I want more.'

'We're working on it,' replied the man with the scar, speaking in pidgin French as the buyer had. 'We'll be in contact.'

The oriental man nodded. He climbed into the passenger seat and buckled himself in. He leaned out to pull the door closed and had an afterthought. 'I'll pay you three thousand US dollars if you bring me a lionskin.'

1
TEAM ALPHA FORCE

Amber Middleton was out of the action and hating it. An ankle sprain suffered while training had put her on crutches, but much worse, it had forced her to pull out of the adventure race through Luangwa National Park, Zambia. She could have been spending three days running, mountain biking, abseiling and horse riding, pushing herself to the limits of endurance with her team-mates Alex, Li, Paulo and Hex. Just the first part alone was like a marathon – a fifty-kilometre run over savannah and into a river gorge. After that there would be more races, just as gruelling.

Gruelling, but fun. Right now, Amber wasn't having much fun. She was sitting in a striped deckchair beside the red Land Rover, wondering whether the neon-yellow bandage on her ankle was really the best colour to offset her ebony skin or whether she should have chosen the Day-Glo green option. Amber was having an easy time while her team-mates battled through a tough course. As well as physical exhaustion they also had to cope with sleep deprivation: the race was non-stop, twenty-four hours a day.

Amber didn't want to be sitting with her feet up, she wanted to be out on the course with her friends.

She was still involved in the race, but it was behind the scenes as the back-up crew with her uncle, John Middleton. They had to follow with vital equipment such as cycle helmets, climbing boots, running shoes, dry socks, medical supplies and food and drink. They dispensed these at transition points – large tents marking where one section of the race ended and another began. The transition point where Amber and John Middleton were waiting now marked the end of the cycling and the start of the hiking and abseiling.

A cluster of competitors appeared out of the dusty landscape. Amber looked up hopefully but it wasn't her team. Although everyone had set off on mountain bikes, this team were now on foot, pushing the bikes, two of the members leaning over the saddles, exhausted. They had slept for only a couple of hours during the thirty-six since the race began; the orange dust that covered them was like a fake suntan. 'Had to walk,' called one of the more awake ones cheerily. 'When I sat in the saddle I kept falling asleep.'

The teams and their back-up crews all wore name patches sewn onto their rucksacks and waterproofs. Amber had TEAM ALPHA FORCE proudly displayed on the front pocket of her shorts. She noticed a spot of mud on it and scratched it off with her fingernail. Never before had the name Alpha Force been seen in public; the five friends had used it only in the presence of a select few such as John Middleton.

Many of the teams in the race had formed just for the event and would disband afterwards, but Alpha Force were more enduring. They trusted one another, quite literally, with their lives. It had started when they were thrown together on a deserted island and had to escape a band of ruthless pirates. At the time, spoilt, beautiful Amber had been mourning her parents' death and hated the whole world. But then she discovered that her folks had had a secret life fighting human rights abuses. What she, Hex, Li, Alex and Paulo went through on the island was like a rebirth, and the five friends had vowed to carry on the Middletons' work. Alpha Force was born, and John Middleton became their anchor man, supplying them with finance and equipment.

The adventure race was an ideal training challenge for Alpha Force, a chance to pit their skills against the best endurance athletes in their age group. It also tested the bonds of a team to the limit. Each team had to finish together, so each member had to keep the others going when all they wanted to do was give up and sleep. Alpha Force were well prepared. As a matter of routine they trained together during every school break, so they functioned as a close-knit unit. When they scattered again to their various schools across the globe, they worked on their fitness and refined their individual skills. Alex lived in the north of England; Amber in Boston, Massachusetts; Paulo in Argentina; Hex in London; and Anglo-Chinese Li lived wherever her zoologist parents were posted.

In training for this event, Paulo had had them all to stay at his parents' ranch, where he had taught them how to handle their mounts both in the saddle and on the ground. Amber, already a keen horse-woman, had howled with laughter at Hex's first efforts. The London boy was a whiz with computers and one of cyberspace's foremost hackers, but was baffled by an animal that completely ignored instructions to stop, go and turn.

Li, an expert in martial arts and free-climbing, had tutored them in abseiling skills during the same trip. Paulo took them to a canyon, and they had watched in awe as Li danced lightly down rock faces that seemed to go on for ever, oblivious to the dizzying drop. Then she had climbed up again, light and sure-footed as a spider on a wall.

Running and cycling they all did every day to

maintain basic fitness, but the star in that department was Alex. Long-limbed and tall, he was built for endurance. Survival was in his blood: his father was a soldier in the SAS and Alex had inherited his relish for challenges in the roughest conditions.

Water sports were Amber's forte, and her privileged upbringing had enabled her to windsurf, water-ski and sail from an early age. Her navigation skills were second to none and would have been of great value in the race as the teams had to find their way from checkpoint to checkpoint through unknown canyons, across savannahs and rivers.

For the last few days of their stay in Argentina, Alpha Force had trained at night, mountain biking up the steep trails that overlooked the plains of Paulo's ranch, climbing, navigating through the endless open spaces, snatching sleep when they could. Then it was back to school for a few weeks, although they kept in e-mail contact to discuss their progress and general strategy for the event. Together Alpha Force were ready for anything the environment could throw at them.

But after all that preparation, Amber had tripped in a pothole while running and sprained her ankle. She had taken plenty of spills in her time and emerged with no more than bruises. This time, however, she had not even been able to get up. She had ripped several ligaments, and healing would take time. She couldn't believe her bad luck.

Amber watched as the other team were given coffee and equipment for the next part of the race. She went back to her book, a text on the languages of Africa. If she couldn't get in on the action, she would at least put the time to good use. Languages were another of her specialities, and she spent long hours studying them in her college library. At least she wasn't missing a real mission, she thought. The race wasn't work, it was play. It wasn't as if it would make a big difference to anyone's life at the end of the day. At least by resting now, she'd be fit and raring to go when a real mission came along.

Out of the corner of her eye she saw one of the competitors sit down and immediately fall asleep, like a robot whose batteries had run out. Even though she could see fatigue was overwhelming him, she felt a pang of envy.

The main objects of Amber's envy – Hex, Paulo, Alex and Li – were also battling fatigue. Seasoned adventure racers had a name for it: fighting the sleep monster.

They were cycling along a dirt track through a wooded area. Every puddle was covered with a swarm of colourful butterflies. Vines curled up the heavy trees, and pads like water lilies sat high in the branches. All four team members wore insect repellent, but mosquitoes and flies still swarmed around their faces.

Alex, setting the pace, kept it steady. They all knew that inexperienced adventure racers made the mistake of going too fast and burning out long before the end. So Alex set a rhythm which the whole team could maintain easily and which would help them cover the distance in good time. Not only did they have to complete the course, they had to spot checkpoints along the way. If they missed one or went the wrong way, many hours would be added to their final score. It was another reason to stay alert and careful.

Hex's job was to remind everyone to eat and drink regularly. He set his watch alarm to bleep every fifteen minutes, and in the meantime looked out for checkpoints and navigated.

Li was in charge of monitoring everyone's physical condition. 'How's everybody feeling?' she called. 'Alex?' They had to give a score out of five.

Li would have said that blond, long-limbed Alex was looking the strongest of them all right now. He pedalled energetically and his face looked animated. 'Four,' he said. But there had been a point an hour before, up a long steep hill, when he had replied, 'Two.' Then Paulo, who had been on five, had taken his pack for a while to give him a chance to recover.

'Hex?' said Li.

Hex looked like he still had energy reserves. His legs pumped the pedals in a sure rhythm and he looked reasonably alert. With a gleam in his green eyes he answered, 'E.'

'What?' said Li, pedalling alongside him.

Hex grinned at her. 'E. The exponential constant.'

'Pardon me, Einstein, but what exactly—?'

'Two point seven one eight two eight. That's about how I'm feeling.'

Alex interjected, 'If he's capable of mathematical jokes, I think he must be at least a pi—'

'Mmm, pie,' said Hex. 'Better than all those fruit bars and biltong we've been eating.' The team carried energy-giving snacks that they could eat on the go, but all of them were now craving a proper meal.

Li turned her attention to the last member of the group. 'Paulo?'

Paulo was behind so Li slowed until she was alongside him. His legs were working on the bike but he was unusually quiet. His brown wavy hair was sticking in sweaty curls to his face and forehead, making him look like a Hispanic cherub, but his eyelids drooped. He didn't answer her.

Li was about to repeat the question when the track took a downward turn. Paulo veered off into the forest.

'Uh-oh, Paulo's asleep,' called Alex.

'Paulo!' yelled Li.

Paulo's bike bounced over the rough ground. His superb sense of balance kept him on board, his legs continuing to travel around in time with the pedals even while asleep so that he looked as though he fully intended the detour.

'He's going to crash into those trees,' cried Hex. He swerved off the track and hared after Paulo. The others followed.

Paulo's bike sliced between two trees and stopped when the handlebars hit the trunks. It stayed there, wedged upright. Paulo didn't move.

Alex reached him first and skidded to a halt, laying his bike on the ground. He peered at his friend's face, expecting to see blood. It was unmarked. Paulo breathed deeply and let out a snore.

Alex turned away in disgust. 'He's still asleep.'

It was the sound of laughing that woke Paulo. He looked around at his friends. His innocent face seemed to be waiting to be told what the joke was and they howled all the more.

Paulo realized. 'Ah,' he said, dismounting from the bike. 'My turn for an unplanned nap?' He pulled the bike clear of the trees, gave it a quick check for damage and pushed it back to the track.

The others followed, pushing their bikes back up through the trees. Hex started to chuckle again and put his hand over his mouth to stop himself. Alex saw and it set him off.

Li wiped a tear from her eye and composed herself. 'Let's go,' she said and picked up her bike.

Amber heard them before she saw them. It was a kind of monotonous chanting. Her four friends were singing. She wasn't quite sure what they were singing, as no tune was discernible, but they were pedalling in time to it. Li's long black hair, braided into a neat plait, swung with the beat like a conductor's baton. Amber filmed them for a few minutes with the team camcorder as they turned the corner. They will be so appalled when they see themselves later, she thought with relish. But for now they were too tired to be embarrassed.

Alex got off his bike and left it where it dropped. He walked around slowly, trying to loosen up after the long hours in the saddle. 'I feel like I've been welded into the shape of a cyclist and I'll never come undone,' he groaned. John Middleton picked up the bike and wheeled it away while Alex walked slowly over to Amber, flexing his legs extravagantly.

She poured him a steaming cup of coffee from a flask. 'You look like a stork, walking like that,' she said.

Alex was watching Paulo, who laid his bike down carefully and sat stiffly on the ground.

'I don't know how Paulo can sit down,' said Alex. 'My backside's on fire.'

Amber searched his face for signs of fatigue. 'You look awake, anyway,' she said.

'With pain like this I certainly am,' replied Alex.

'Just keep walking around,' said John Middleton, coming back for Paulo's bike.

Amber hobbled over to Paulo and poured him coffee. '*Gracias*,' he said, and gave her a big smile. He looked remarkably relaxed and laid-back, thought Amber, but then he always managed to look like that. How did he do it?

Li and Hex had sat down to undo their shoes, one-handed, each nursing a coffee cup. They were moving very slowly, so tired that drinking coffee and untying trainers at the same time was almost too much to cope with.

Amber grabbed the medical kit and got to work. 'Show me your blisters,' she said briskly. She kneeled in front of Hex and inspected his bare feet. He already had a large, raw blister from running and now it looked worse. Amber tipped antiseptic onto a ball of cotton wool and dabbed it on. Hex jumped as though he'd had an electric shock.

Amber grinned sadistically. 'You still awake?'

Hex nodded sleepily. 'Yes, thanks.'

'So what have I missed?' said Amber.

'Er . . .' Hex tried to remember but it was too much trouble. 'I'll tell you later.'

While Amber inspected Li's blisters, John Middleton handed round hiking boots and abseiling helmets, and restocked their backpacks with snacks. Within minutes, Team Alpha Force were back on their feet and marching away.

'God, I feel like an ancient parent,' said Amber as she watched them leave.

* * *

'So how's everyone doing?' said Li.

'You've just asked us that!' exclaimed Hex.

'Sorry,' mumbled Li. The exhaustion had crept up on her and now she felt more tired than she could ever remember. She was barely even aware of putting one foot in front of the other.

Paulo came up behind her and took hold of the shoulder straps of her pack. 'Let me take this for a while and I'll do the monitoring now.'

Li gratefully unfastened the belt of her pack and let Paulo carry it – part of good teamwork was not just giving help, but knowing when to accept it. Then it was back to concentrating on one foot in front of the other.

Alex saw how tired she was. 'Hold onto my pack for a while,' he said. Li nodded and hooked her hand into a loop on the side of the rucksack. That felt a bit easier; like being towed. That was the challenge of these races, she told herself. You hit an absolute low, but if you kept fed and hydrated it would pass. In an hour she might feel fine.

They walked up a steep hill, passing another team, who were sitting in a row along the path having a furious argument about where to go next. But Team Alpha Force were sure of where the abseiling point was and carried on up.

The sun was beginning to set and the land dropped away on one side to give a spectacular view. Grasslands stretched as far as the eye could see. Oxbow lakes glittered in the golden sunlight. A river snaked through the parched land, and beyond it, the wildlife of Africa was laid out in a panorama. Vast herds of wildebeest, springbok, buffalo and zebra moved like ants across the plain. The four friends walked in awestruck silence.

Even Li emerged from her cocoon of half-sleep as they climbed. 'Wow,' she said quietly, letting Alex pull her along.

'This must be the abseil point,' said Hex. Lines of rope were attached to rings driven into a wall of rock and snaked over the edge. 'Who's going first?'

'I'll go last,' said Li. 'You guys get down.'

The next Li knew, voices were shouting her name. She came to with a start. She must have sat down and zoned out, although she didn't remember it. Now she understood how Paulo had dozed on the bike. She hadn't even realized she was falling asleep.

She went close to the edge and peered over. Hex, Paulo and Alex were standing at the bottom, waving; Alex was holding up the harness. They had already made their descent. Li nodded and picked up the rope at her end. As she hoisted up the harness she sized up the rock face. It was long and straight; no sharp projections or hazards, just a fabulous sense of sky and sandy rock. Li was feeling better already.

She pulled the harness over the edge and clambered in.

Down below, Paulo, Hex and Alex watched her fasten the harness and pull on the rope to test it.

'Now we'll see how it's meant to be done,' grinned Hex. Any moment her slight figure would skip lightly down the cliff.

'Bet we look like three baby elephants compared with Li,' agreed Alex.

But Li stayed up at the top, not moving.

Paulo grinned. 'Do you think she's fallen asleep? She's hit a tired patch.'

'That beats you for weird sleeping places,' said Hex. 'Li,' he called out, 'are you still with us?'

Li turned to look down at them.

'She looks awake,' said Alex.

Paulo frowned. 'Something's wrong,' he said to himself under his breath. He called out, 'Li, are you OK?'

They watched as she glanced down and gave a thumbs-up sign, then turned back to what she was doing. But still she did not move. The harness showed up bright purple against her slim-fitting black cycle shorts and T-shirt and they could see by the way it hung that she had not yet committed her weight to it. She stood looking intently at her hands holding onto the rope.

Paulo's spine tingled. Something was very wrong. 'I think she's frozen up there,' he said. He shook his head; had he really said that? Was he dreaming?

Hex and Alex both looked at him in astonishment.

'Never,' said Alex vehemently.

'Not Li,' added Hex. 'She'll be on her way in a minute.'

But she wasn't. She remained standing at the edge of the cliff, looking down at her two hands on the rope.

'She has definitely frozen,' said Paulo again.

'I'm feeling quite strong at the moment,' said Hex. 'I could go back and help her . . .' His voice trailed off as he saw the expressions on the faces of his two friends. 'Wouldn't go down well, would it?'

'Probably not,' said Alex. He stared up at Li, willing her to move.

Another team had arrived at the top. Suddenly, Li stepped backwards. The harness took her weight. It was the fastest abseil Alex had ever seen. Li hurried down the cliff face as though the hounds of hell were after her. What had happened to the poised, confident climber who had danced down cliff faces in Argentina all day long?

She landed at the base of the cliff and stepped out of the harness. The moment she let it go it was whisked back up to the top, brushing a hail of pebbles and sand down the rock face.

'Li, are you OK?' said Paulo. 'What happened up there?'

Li's face was grim. 'I'm tired, that's all. Next checkpoint is this way, isn't it?' She set off at a determined march.

Paulo, Alex and Hex glanced at each other. Li looked angry with herself. They had to jog to keep up with her.

Paulo tried to lighten the mood. 'What embarrassing things we do when we're tired, eh? It'll be Hex and Alex's turn next.'

2
KILLERS

The shots rang out, sending birds screeching into the sky, where the last rays of sun were sinking away for the day. The elephant screamed, curling her trunk as she blasted out a warning. Her eyes showed white with fear. Blood streamed from the holes in her head. She screamed again, a pink froth foaming from her mouth.

One of the poachers squinted into the growing darkness. The ugly scar on his cheek crinkled like a grotesque second mouth. He fired again, aiming high on the head. The elephant keeled over and sank against a large rock, thrashing the sandy surface with her trunk.

She tried to rise but crashed back to the ground. The man with the scarred face jumped backwards, his weapon ready to fire again. But the elephant was losing the battle. The ugly holes in her head leaked blood, spreading quickly into the crazy paving of her crackly skin. It flowed down onto her tusks, turning them from gleaming white to sticky ruby.

The scarred man and his poacher companions watched as her life leaked out onto the sandy soil.

Soon the elephant's only movement was the heaving of her great sides as she fought to keep breathing. Her trunk flailed like a blind, dying snake. Wide streaks of moisture ran out of her eyes like tears.

The man with the yellow bandanna put his weapon on the ground and picked up his machete. 'I reckon it's not going to fight much longer.' He wiped sand from his eyes with the back of his hand. They had to get to work and remove the tusks as quickly as possible.

The man who wore the hyena tooth kept his

AK-47 at the ready. Rangers patrolled the game park and you never knew when one was about to appear.

A loud trumpeting sounded. The poachers looked at each other in alarm. Elephants live in extended family groups, and defend their cousins and sisters as fiercely as they would their children. 'I thought this one was on its own,' hissed Scarface.

They heard the sound again, and with it the crash of breaking foliage. It came from behind the great bulk of the dying elephant. The poachers grabbed their guns. They weren't about to leave their spoils without a fight.

A baby elephant trotted around the rock, its trunk high, ears flapping backwards and forwards. It let out another scream.

'Leave it,' said the man with the yellow bandanna, lowering his weapon and leaning it against a tree. 'It's on its own. We've got to get to work.' He picked up his machete and approached the dead mother elephant.

Scarface didn't lower his weapon. 'It's drawing attention to us. We can't take the chance.' His scar twitched.

The baby elephant slowed. Its steps became hesitant. It approached the body of its mother and reached cautiously towards her with its trunk, the sensitive end fidgeting like fingers. It touched her, stroking the hide. After a few moments it was still, resting the tip of its trunk on her head.

Li walked ahead of the others, maintaining the same fast pace she had set when she started off from the foot of the cliff. She was fatigued but she would not allow it to show. She would not let the team down again. She refused even to think about what had happened on the cliff. The sun had just set and as she walked she pulled her fleece out of her pack, wriggling in and out of her rucksack straps so that she could put it on while walking.

The next checkpoint was over a sturdy road bridge. It took them into the area they had seen from the cliff top. They stopped for a moment to put on head torches and Hex got out the bear banger, a metal tube that fired cartridges and made a noise like a firework. They had been told the wildlife should stay away from a big group if they kept together and made a noise, but just in case it didn't, they could light the bear banger to scare anything off. Paulo kept his torch in his hand, and shone it on the ground to check for snakes.

The river stretched out wide beside them, making gentle lapping sounds.

'That's the Luangwa,' said Alex. 'It flows from Tanzania into the Zambezi, and then into the Indian Ocean. Wow.' He was talking half to himself. Although he felt alert, he had missed nearly two nights' sleep and nothing seemed real. The darkness outside the narrow arc of his head torch seemed to go on for ever. Occasionally there was a splash as something large moved in the water – a crocodile or a hippo. Li had picked a path ten metres from the river edge to keep them at a safe distance.

They crossed a clear track in the grass. It was a game trail, a path worn down by animals going to the river and back. Paulo stopped and directed his torch down onto it. He gasped in wonder. 'Look!'

Alex and Hex peered over his shoulder, the beams

from their lamps merging like a spotlight. Paulo had found a heavy four-toed print.

Li gave it a glance. 'Hippo. Keep off its trail or it'll panic and go for you.'

'That's nice,' said Paulo. 'I thought hippos were cuddly.'

'They're not,' replied Li. She marched on.

Paulo shrugged. Li was usually even more fascinated by the animal world than he was. She was probably tired, or maybe she was still worried by what had happened at the cliff. He wanted to say to her, *Don't worry, we're all doing strange things in this race – because we haven't had any sleep.* But this clearly wasn't the time or the place.

It wasn't long before they came to another game trail. Paulo stopped and flicked his torch over it. 'More big feet,' he said, delighted. 'Looks like skid marks with three huge toes.'

Li glanced at it. 'Rhino,' she said, without much interest.

But Paulo found the endless variety of tracks fascinating. He found little ones like dainty points, which Li said were made by a tiny antelope called a dik-dik. Hex and Alex caught his enthusiasm, walking along for most of the time with their torches pointed at the ground.

Paulo found some broad, heavy tracks.

'Lone buffalo,' said Li grimly. 'Good job it's not going our way; we'd be stuffed.'

Alex decided it was time to cheer Li up. He stopped and pointed out another track. 'Li, what's this?'

She looked down. Alex was pointing at a deep track made by a mountain-bike tyre.

Li looked at the track for a moment and then a smile made its way slowly across her face. 'That, you dunderhead, is an elephant riding a unicycle.' She walked on, shaking her head.

The others followed. Soon it was time for Paulo to check everyone's physical condition.

'I feel two point seven five,' said Hex.

'Three-ish,' said Alex.

'Four,' replied Li.

'What's that?' Hex stopped and stood stock-still, listening. 'Did anyone hear that?'

They all halted. Above the ticking of the insects there was a long, mournful sound from the river.

'No, not that,' said Hex. 'That's a humpback whale playing the tuba.'

Alex and Paulo laughed.

Li said, 'It's a hippo.'

Hex was still listening. 'There,' he said. 'I think it was a scream.'

'Baboons. Come on, we'd better keep moving.'

And then they all heard it. The voice was unmistakably human. The word it cried out was also unmistakable: '*Help!*'

Alex called out, 'Hello? Where are you? Shout again.'

The sound came again, loud and desperate. It was close.

'Over there,' said Paulo. He turned towards it.

The voice called out again: 'Careful! There's a pit.' A figure came towards them, rustling through the grass, the headlamp held low in his hand and bobbing as he ran.

'Tessa's hurt,' he gasped. His accent was South African. He wore a badge – CHRIS, TEAM SPITFIRE – and a red sweat band around his head. 'Are you the organizers?' Before any of them could answer, he turned and started running, his bobbing torch leading the way. 'They're coming,' he called.

Team Alpha Force gave chase. Paulo, in front, was the first to see what the problem was. His torch grazed a mass of pointed stakes in a shallow pit. He stopped at once. The torch beam found a tangle of grass and branches. The desperate face of a girl flinched away from the light.

'A poacher's trap,' said Alex. He took his head lamp off and flashed it around. 'There's the bait – look.' In one corner lay the roughly cut haunch of some dark animal, the cloven hoof still intact and rimmed with a fine ring of white hair.

Paulo got carefully down into the pit. He was the team medic – another skill honed during his long years of treating injured animals on his parents' ranch.

The frightened girl was breathing hard and sweat was running down her face, mingling with her tears. She was wearing a fleece but it was damp with sweat and she was shivering. Paulo took his fleece off and put it around her shoulders.

'I didn't see it. We must have gone off course a bit. I just fell.' Her voice was weak.

'Hush,' said Paulo. 'Everything's going to be fine.'
It was when he ran the torch over her that he saw
the damage. At first it looked as though Tessa was
just sitting in the pit with one leg extended
awkwardly before her. Then he realized that one of
the stakes had been driven deeply into the back of her
knee. Blood had coursed down her leg and the stake
in a sticky black river. Her shorts were soaked too.
The pit must have been disguised to look like solid
ground. She must have walked straight onto it and
crashed through, impaling her leg as she fell.

Hex, Li and Alex watched from the edge of the pit.
Hex was glad of the darkness; as Paulo's light picked
out the wound he was sure he had turned green.

Paulo looked closely at the girl's injury. The blood
seemed to be oozing rather than coming in spurts,
which suggested it was from a vein and not an artery.
That was good. However, the bleeding hadn't
stopped, and that was not good. And the stake
might have pierced the joint, which was even worse.

Tessa fixed him with desperate eyes. 'Get this out
of me.' Her voice rasped.

Paulo spoke gently. 'We shouldn't do that. We

34

should get you to safety. That stake is probably stopping you from losing too much blood. We can move you with it.' But he didn't let her know what he was really thinking: if the stake was removed there was a chance she might bleed to death.

Alex spoke to Chris. 'How long has she been here like this?'

'An hour – two hours maybe,' said Chris.

'Where's the rest of your team?' said Hex.

Chris's voice was defensive. 'They were being idiots so we decided to let them cool off on their own for a while.'

Alex too was glad of the cover of darkness. It meant Chris couldn't see his undisguised look of astonishment. Going off on your own in an area like this was sheer lunacy; teams had to stick together. 'So no-one knows you're here?' he said.

'They were bound to come past soon,' said Chris. 'We were going to meet just before the next checkpoint.'

Paulo looked up from tending Tessa's wound. 'Can one of you guys have a look at these stakes? See how we're going to get it out.'

'No problem,' said Li. She stepped down into the pit.

Hex unscrewed the cap on his water bottle and passed it down to Tessa. 'Drink some water; you need fluids.'

Tessa grabbed it with both hands. 'Thanks,' she whispered.

Li pulled at one of the sharpened stakes in the pit. She thought she would be able to move it easily, but it had been hammered in deep. She had to give up. 'I can't budge it.'

'Here, I'll help,' said Alex. He jumped down beside her. He grasped one of the stakes and pulled back, using all his weight, as though he was working a giant lever. The stake loosened a little but not much. He paused for breath.

Li grasped the post. 'Let's try together, One . . . two . . . three . . .' They pulled backwards.

'Now push forwards,' said Alex. 'It's coming.'

Finally the post came out. Alex and Li both doubled over, catching their breath. Their head torches illuminated the base of the stake. 'Look at the depth of that,' said Alex. 'No wonder it didn't come out easily.'

They heard the rasp of Tessa's voice. 'The poachers hammer them in like that so they don't fall over when a heavy animal lands in them.' She winced as she spoke. 'I live in a game reserve.'

Paulo bit his lip. The stake Tessa was impaled on was just as deep in the ground. If they yanked it about like that they would cause her unbearable pain. What were they going to do?

Then the sound came. A deep roar, out in the darkness.

Everyone froze: Paulo, his light inspecting the base of the stake; Alex and Li, about to get out of the pit; Hex, digging for medical supplies in his rucksack; Tessa, slumped in pain; Chris, watching them.

'That was a lion,' said Li. 'And it's very close.'

3
RESCUE

Chris's voice was hushed, as though he was afraid the lions could hear him. 'They've been sniffing around ever since Tessa fell. They know someone's injured. We used that bear banger thing but they kept coming back. Now we've used all our cartridges.'

'Lions can smell blood from miles away,' said Li. 'And they hunt at night.'

'We'd better rethink our plan,' said Alex. He climbed out of the pit. 'We can't take Tessa out through those hungry lions. But the last checkpoint is only about ten minutes away. I could go for help—'

'You can't go on your own,' said Li. 'I'll come.' She vaulted out of the pit.

'I'll stay and help Paulo,' said Hex. 'If we stay close to the stakes they should give us a bit of protection.' He grabbed Chris's sleeve. 'Chris, you get in too.'

As Chris looked around, Hex felt him suddenly go rigid. He stood stock-still, staring into the dark beyond the pit. 'Look,' he said softly.

Alex followed the line of Chris's torch. A pair of eyes looked back at him from the blackness, reflecting like mirrors.

Alex spoke quietly. 'Hex, have you got the bear banger? I think we'd better set it off.'

'Good idea,' said Hex. 'Cover your ears, everyone.'

Hex lit the banger. A loud explosion split the night. Tessa jumped as though it had gone off underneath her, then gave a sob of pain.

Her nerves are shot to hell, thought Paulo. He patted her arm gently.

Alex, Hex and Li peered into the gloom, sweeping their head torches from side to side.

'I think it's gone,' said Alex. 'We ought to get going now. We can run there in—'

'We mustn't run,' interrupted Li. 'If there's a lion watching we could trigger its kill response. We've got to walk.'

Alex swallowed. 'Great,' he said.

'Take this,' said Hex. He passed over the bear banger and the remaining two cartridges.

'Surely we need to keep it with us,' protested Chris. 'We're sitting targets.'

'We'll probably be OK if we stay in the pit,' said Paulo. 'There are quite a few of us and if we make a lot of noise we can probably keep the lions away.' He looked at Li and Alex. 'You take the bear banger.'

Alex took his compass out of his rucksack and began to get a bearing. Normally he carried it in the survival kit he kept on his belt, but the rules of the race were very strict about what equipment was allowed. Even Hex had had to leave his most precious possession behind with Amber: a state-of-the-art palmtop computer. They weren't even allowed mobile phones or radios because back-up crew might use them to help their teams navigate, which would be cheating. That's why the course included so many checkpoints – to ensure the contestants were safe and well and coping with all the challenges.

Li swept her torch around the undergrowth again. 'We seem to be clear. Let's go.' She turned away.

'We'll be back as soon as we can,' Alex called over his shoulder.

Hex, Paulo and Chris watched their lights bob away into the darkness and heard their voices fade. Soon they could hear only the night sounds of insects and the cries of far-off animals. They were on edge as they listened, expecting another blood-chilling roar.

Tessa's weak voice rasped, 'Have the lions gone?'

Paulo tried to sound reassuring. 'They're usually scared of people, and there are lots of us here to stop them coming near you.' But he knew that these days, some lions had lost their fear of humans. He hoped these hadn't.

'Yes, I know,' said Tessa. 'I grew up with them, remember?'

Paulo smiled sheepishly. She probably also knew what he'd left unsaid too.

Tessa noticed. 'I'm very glad you're here,' she said quietly. 'You're a lot more use than certain other people I could mention.' Her voice had an edge, despite her weakness. 'Tell me something – if the medics can't get this stake out of my leg, what will they do?'

'Don't you worry about that,' said Hex. 'They'll know how to get it out.'

Tessa muttered. It sounded like: 'No they won't,' but none of them realized what she was about to do. Suddenly she jerked backwards, drawing her leg up violently. A guttural groan came from deep in her throat.

'Tessa, no!' cried Paulo.

With a ferocious cry the girl pulled her leg off the stake.

Blood spurted furiously from the wound as the artery began to pump. A bright red jet hit Paulo on the cheek. Hex whipped a large, absorbent field dressing out of the medical kit and clamped it down hard on Tessa's leg. Tessa squirmed and writhed with pain, oblivious to his attempts to help her.

Hex hung on. 'Keep still, Tessa,' he called. 'I need to stop the bleeding.'

The blood soaked the pad in no time. It pulsed up between Hex's fingers like a sticky geyser.

'Paulo!' he shouted. 'Tie a tourniquet.'

A roar welled out of the darkness.

Chris's light flashed off the trees as he scanned the undergrowth in panic. 'They're back,' he said. Anxiety made his voice high. 'Tessa, why did you do that? You've made the lions come back.'

Paulo and Hex could see nothing but Tessa's blood. Hex's face and T-shirt were splattered, the pad was sodden. He had all his weight on it, but Tessa's leg was jerking and the pad was in danger of slipping off.

Paulo went for the nearest thing that would make a tourniquet. Hex's eyes opened wide in surprise as his friend's hands lunged towards his waist. Paulo grabbed Hex's belt buckle, unfastened it and whipped the whole thing out of his shorts in two seconds flat. He wrapped it around the top of Tessa's thigh and pulled it tight.

Hex felt the throbbing under the dressings start to slow. 'It's working, Paulo,' he said. 'Keep it tight.'

Gradually, the flow of blood stopped. Tessa lay quietly. She looked exhausted.

'I'll secure the tourniquet,' said Paulo. 'Can you put another dressing on that?' He looked at his watch; every ten minutes he'd have to remember to loosen the tourniquet and retighten it, otherwise Tessa could get gangrene. He looked round to see Chris standing up in the pit, sweeping his torch around the undergrowth. Then he sat down again. He looked terrified.

Paulo stood up. 'Anything?'

Chris's teeth were bared in fear. 'I can't believe you let them take the bear banger.'

Paulo let the remark pass. An argument wouldn't do any good. It was far more important to see if there really *was* anything out there. 'Sit down,' he said. Chris did as he was told; he was too scared not to.

Paulo looked into the darkness. There was enough undergrowth to provide several lions with plenty of cover, even in broad daylight. Then, in the beam of his torch, a mere five metres away, he saw a lioness.

She was completely still, like a picture taken in mid stride, front paw lifted. She was gazing at the group intently. Paulo tried flicking the torch beam back and forth across her eyes. She didn't flinch, but stared back. Paulo could see the texture of her nose, the outline of her mouth like a rim of black leather, the way her sandy fur faded to white on her muzzle, the open jaws that revealed a red flash of tongue and the jagged outline of teeth.

Chris stood up. Paulo swiftly moved his torch away from the lioness so that Chris wouldn't see her – he was bound to panic. 'Sit down, Chris,' he said. 'There's nothing there. Come on, guys, let's make a bit of noise.'

Alex and Li were making good progress. They retraced their steps down to the path they had been following, and onto the track. Soon they were passing over the game trails they'd seen earlier.

'There's the rhino track,' said Li. She was talking partly to herself, to convince herself they didn't have much further to go. The torch on her head was creating a tunnel effect, making her feel sleepy again. The grassy track in front of her looked neverending, like a pattern designed to put you in a trance.

Alex caught the weariness in her voice. 'Take the torch off your head, then you don't get that weird effect,' he said. 'It was driving me mad too.'

Li slipped the headband off and wrapped it around her hand. Alex was right, that did feel better. 'Good thinking,' she said. 'That's—'

A sound exploded from the bush. Li grabbed Alex and gripped his arm hard, her nails digging in like claws. All he could hear was a frenzy of roaring, savage and purposeful, out there in the dark. And it was very close.

'It's lions hunting,' whispered Li. 'Over by the river.'

They heard scrabbling – a fight? There was a high-pitched sound like a howl; then its answer, a deep, forbidding roar. More voices joined in. How many of them were there?

'I'll get this thing ready,' said Alex. He prepared to light the bear banger.

'Don't use it yet,' said Li urgently. 'We might not need to. It sounds like they've made the kill and now they're all gathering to eat it. We should be able to get past without them bothering us if we stay well away. If we upset them, though, we'll be in more trouble. They're really hyped up when they've made a kill.'

'Are you sure?' said Alex. He flashed his torch around. He could see nothing but darkness and foliage. It made the noises all the more horrible.

'Sort of,' said Li. 'Just keep that bear banger ready.'

They marched on. Behind them, the roaring gave way to fighting and snarling. 'Now they'll start to squabble over who eats what,' said Li.

It was a chilling sound, vicious and primeval.

Gradually, the noise of the lions faded into the distance. Adrenaline stopped pumping through Alex's veins and he felt a wave of fatigue. It was extreme, like having a blanket dropped over his head. Not now, he said to himself. He gripped the handle of the bear banger hard, feeling its ridged handle dig into his palm. Maybe that would keep him awake.

But he had been on the move for more than two days and nights. He had to try not to think about it. He couldn't believe that his body was craving sleep here, among all these hunting lions. Do it for the others, he told himself. They were depending on him to bring help.

'Paulo, don't fall asleep,' said Hex. He caught Paulo by the shoulders and shook him urgently. 'We mustn't fall asleep.'

Paulo was sitting next to Tessa. His head had nodded onto his chest for a moment. He came to with a jolt. '*Dios*,' he muttered to himself. He hadn't realized he was dozing. A shiver turned his spine to ice. A lion could so easily have crept up on them.

Hex checked Tessa. 'The tourniquet seems all right. Where's Chris?'

Paulo shone his torch around. Chris was slumped in a corner, his head burrowed into the side of the pit like a hibernating creature. Paulo turned to Hex and said quietly, 'I reckon he's better like that.'

As Paulo swung the torch back, he caught sight of a pair of eyes up on the rim of the pit. 'Lion,' he said simply. A huge face, surrounded by a mane, was staring back at him.

Hex's foot touched something. It was the bait the poachers had left. Hex picked it up by its hoof. 'Mind out,' he said to Paulo and hurled it at the lion. The lion whirled round and trotted after it.

'Nice one,' said Paulo. The lion stopped a few metres away. He sniffed the meat and settled to gnaw it.

'That won't keep it amused for very long,' said Hex.

Suddenly they heard a noise. Relief flooded through Hex's veins like a ray of light. 'Hey, that's a vehicle.'

A powerful set of headlights swung through the trees. Hex and Paulo stood on tiptoe in the pit and waved. They saw the solid front of a Range Rover. Its bonnet bore the red cross of the medics. With a squeal of brakes it pulled up beside the pit.

Alex and Li jumped out, along with three paramedics.

'She's over there,' said Li.

One paramedic ran past her and dropped down

into the pit beside Tessa. He took one look at her and called up to his colleague: 'Get the stretcher.'

Chris woke and stood up, rubbing his eyes as he made his way to the edge of the pit.

Paulo and Hex climbed wearily out. 'You made it,' said Paulo to Alex.

Alex nodded over at the undergrowth. Just beyond where their torches had been able to reach were three more lions, only twelve metres away, sitting on their haunches and staring at the group.

'Looks like we were just in time,' said Li.

4
TO THE BITTER END

The transition point was bustling with horses, riders and helpers. Competitors were starting to come back from the mounted orienteering phase of the race.

Paulo, Hex, Li and Alex walked their horses in and jumped off. It was mid-morning the next day. They had completed another section in good time and it was all change again.

Tessa had been taken to hospital and Team Alpha Force had voted unanimously to continue despite the detour. There was still a race to complete. So Li, Alex, Hex and Paulo had hiked to the next checkpoint, taken a two-hour break for sleep, and met Amber for the next phase – the thirty-kilometre orienteering ride. Now they were back, having successfully persuaded their mounts through rivers and over mountain passes.

John Middleton grabbed the two friskier horses and led them away to untack and rub them down. Amber laid her crutches down on the ground and hopped up to take the quieter ones. But as she led them away they jogged with their tails in the air and eyes wide, staring at the strange bouncing creature that had taken charge of them. Amber realized she had made a mistake. Far from being tired and docile, they thought she wanted to play.

She pulled one of them up hard. It stood still, shocked. She sprang off her good leg up onto its back. The saddle immediately felt like home. 'Right,' she said. She gave the horse she was on a strong squeeze with her thighs, and firmly held the reins of the other one. 'Now I'm up here you'll do as you're told.' The horses quietened down immediately.

As she took the horses to the washing-down area, a truck trundled slowly past. It bore a logo: TEAM

WOLF. Three competitors were lolling together on the back seats, fast asleep like children. Amber stared. The teams weren't allowed into their back-up vehicles so they must have withdrawn. But Team Wolf were legendary in adventure-racing circles. All around her, Amber was beginning to see how the course had taken its toll. Team Alpha Force were proving themselves in one of the toughest sports on earth.

This next phase was the final one – an eight-kilometre sprint. In normal circumstances that was a negligible distance for Alpha Force. At the start of the race they had agreed that this was where they would make up any lost time or mistakes. But now, after days of constant slog, it seemed a different prospect.

Paulo slipped off his riding boots and protective chaps. He picked up his running shoes but could hardly bear to put them on.

Alex, his chaps discarded where they had fallen, was already tying his laces. If they kept a positive frame of mind they would finish in good time. 'We'll get straight out and do the final push now, OK?' he said. His voice was strong.

Hex felt as if he was dead on his feet but he forced himself to match Alex's upbeat tone. 'No time to lose,' he replied.

Li straightened up. 'We're not tired, are we? Other people have given up but we won't. We've come through the worst and soon it will be over.'

'Everyone ready?' said Paulo. 'Then let's go.'

They set off, jogging in a row at a good fast pace.

Amber took care of her horses and made her way back to the Land Rover. She checked her watch. Time for her insulin. Amber was a diabetic and had to carry insulin with her in a hi-tech injecting pen to take twice a day, but that didn't cramp her style.

As she prepared to give herself the injection in her thigh she was aware of eyes on her. Someone from one of the other back-up teams was watching her, his face curious and pitying. Amber gave herself the dose, then stared pointedly at the man. He quickly looked away, but Amber was annoyed. She felt like saying, *No, I'm not an invalid or ill. I'm a fully active, fully functioning member of Alpha Force.*

As she put away the injection pen, John Middleton

came back from the stabling area, brushing hay off his clothes. 'We're allowed to follow the teams for the last phase,' he said. 'Shall we go?'

'Good idea,' said Amber.

The course took them out onto an unmade road. A team had just set out, running slowly with laboured steps. The road stretched ahead, long and straight; to either side, scrubby grass grew. It was a monotonous view with no landmarks.

'Oh, that is nasty,' said Amber. 'That's a real test of endurance – it's so tedious.'

John Middleton was having to keep his foot steadily on the gas pedal. 'It's uphill too. Even worse.'

He overtook the runners by swerving onto the grass and bumping over the rough ground. As the Land Rover passed them Amber saw their exhausted faces, locked in their own private hell. 'This is a real killer,' she said, 'especially after all they've done before.'

They passed another team, who had slowed to a walk. 'That bunch look beat,' said John.

Amber spotted Team Alpha Force. 'There they are!'

They were walking, heads down, determined. Paulo, Li and Hex had linked arms, with Alex walking on his own, but their pace had slackened since they'd set out. 'That does not look good,' muttered Amber.

'And there's the finish,' said John. In the distance, about two kilometres away, was a crowd of people gathered around two flagpoles supporting a fluorescent yellow banner.

In front of Alpha Force were another team. A Land Cruiser crawled along beside them. A figure leaned out of the window, waving and yelling at them.

Amber grabbed the rule book, which was sitting on the dashboard. 'Are they allowed to do that?' She riffled through the pages. 'Aha, here we are. "During the last phase only, members of the back-up team may accompany the competing team, in vehicles or on foot, and are permitted to offer encouragement and training tips. They must not, however, touch the teams in any way." So long as we don't give them a lift or tow them, we can do anything we want.' She threw the rule book back on the dashboard and grabbed her crutches, which were propped in the passenger footwell. 'Uncle, stop the car.'

John Middleton braked in a cloud of dust and looked at her quizzically.

'Guys, I'm hallucinating,' said Hex. A slim black girl on crutches had just come out of nowhere and was now alongside him. What's more, she was grinning at him.

'Hi,' said Amber. Her teeth were brilliant white and her eyes glittered.

'Guys, I'm having a nightmare,' groaned Hex.

Paulo finally registered what was happening. His reactions were so slow he felt like a sloth coming to.

Alex was staring at his feet, putting one in front of the other. He looked up momentarily. 'Hi, Amber.' His voice was groggy.

Li mumbled hello.

Amber kept up with them easily, poling herself along on the crutches as though she was punting a boat along a river. 'Hex,' she said, 'move your ass.'

Hex looked at her distastefully. 'Oh no, it's Miss Motivator. Go away.'

Amber looked at the team in front of them. One of them had fallen over. Now was the chance for Alpha Force. 'Hex,' she said, 'if I beat you to the finish there will be hell to pay.' She took off at a surprising speed, the crutches allowing her to vault over the ground in long strides.

Hex's arm was still linked around Li's. He disengaged. 'Well, I won't be beaten by someone on crutches,' he muttered, and took off in pursuit.

The judge, looking through binoculars from the finish line, could not believe his eyes. A girl on crutches was powering past the leading team, and turning to shout at someone behind her. Team Alpha Force found a burst of energy and began to run. They ran past the leaders, Team Hunter, pursuing the girl on crutches like greyhounds chasing a hare.

The trainer in the Land Cruiser gave his team a loud wake-up call. 'Come on, Hunters!' He was leaning so far out of the window that he was in danger of falling out. Team Hunter suddenly came to life. They began to run, fast.

At the finish line, Amber stopped and looked back. Team Hunter were gaining. She suddenly recognized their trainer: it was the man who had been staring at her when she took her insulin. She remembered the look of pity on his face. She opened her lungs and gave a great bellow. 'Move it, Alpha Force!'

Team Hunter had caught up. The teams were neck and neck. Eight runners in a row, pounding out the last hundred metres of their extraordinary marathon.

'Come on!' shouted the Hunters' trainer.

Hex, Li, Paulo and Alex were running hard. Their legs were on fire and their lungs were bursting. But the finishing line was merely ten or twenty strides ahead. After all they had gone through, Alpha Force were not going to give anything less than their best. Alex was the first to put on a spurt, and when he did, the others found reserves they had not dreamed existed. Adrenaline gave them raw power. Little by little, they drew ahead of the other team, intent only on reaching Amber – and at that moment a great cheer went up.

They had done it. They had finished their first adventure race – and in fine style.

Li, Paulo, Alex and Hex sat on the tarpaulin floor tent at the finish, their bare feet in bowls of warm water. All around were exhausted, relieved athletes who had finished the course, nursing their wounds while the results were calculated.

'Oh that feels good,' said Hex, wriggling his toes. 'I'm not going to wear shoes for days.'

'What I want right now,' said Li, 'is a huge plate of chips with mayonnaise. And I never want to see another fruit bar or packet of nuts.'

'I want a steak with garlic butter,' said Paulo.

'I second that,' said Alex. 'In fact, I'll have two.'

Amber was on her way back from the Land Rover, the medical kit in a red bag over her shoulder. Picking her way through the throng of bodies was like walking across a crowded beach – especially difficult with crutches. People took up so much room when they sat down. And why did they all put their hands on the floor?

She reached the others and dropped to her knees,

lowering the medical kit to the ground. 'Doctor's here,' she said briskly. She brought out the bottle of antiseptic and a pad of cotton wool. 'Who's first?' Her mouth split into a grin of pure sadism.

'There's your uncle,' said Li.

From their seated position, John Middleton looked even taller than he actually was. He grinned at them. 'I've got your results. Out of forty teams that started, only twenty completed. So you've already done well to be sitting here in this tent. And . . .' He paused.

Five faces looked back at him. They were hanging on his every word.

'Spit it out, Uncle,' said Amber. 'It's been a long day.'

'You made no mistakes at the checkpoints, no mistakes in navigation, you got time penalties in the abseiling and hiking phase but I'm working on the judges about that because of the mitigating circumstances . . . you were first in the final sprint and . . . third overall . . .'

His voice was drowned in the cheer that followed. Water bowls went flying as the five all grabbed each other in a gigantic, boisterous hug. 'Oh,' added John Middleton, 'and you were voted friendliest team in the race.'

'That must have been you, Li,' said Paulo. 'You'll bat your eyelashes at anything—' His words became a splutter as Li upended the one surviving water bowl over his head.

'It can't have been you, Amber,' Hex was saying. 'You've been like a bear with a sore head.'

'I still beat you to the finish,' retorted Amber, picking up her crutch and poking him in the ribs. Hex grabbed it and yanked hard, and she fell over on top of him with a shriek, then rolled onto her back laughing.

'Listen, guys,' said John Middleton, 'I've got to go and see to something. But you should take this up properly. There are teams that do this semi-professionally. You'd be world class in no time.' His voice was serious.

Amber propped herself up on one elbow, frowning. 'But Uncle, that's not what Alpha Force is about.'

'Yeah,' said Alex. 'How would that help anyone?'

John Middleton spread his hands as though what he was about to say was a great revelation. 'Raising money for charity. You could do a lot of good like that. Think about it.' He looked at his watch. 'I've got to dash. See you later.' He raised his hand in a wave as he moved away.

Amber watched him go and let out an exasperated sigh. 'That's typical of my uncle. Now he's going to be finding us nice safe competitions instead of proper work. I don't want to be an athlete; I want to solve real problems.'

Alex lay flat beside her and closed his eyes. 'Then we do what we always do. We find our own missions.'

'Hear, hear,' said Hex, prodding his blister. Li and Paulo murmured in agreement.

'Team Alpha Force?' called a voice. A figure wearing a steward's T-shirt was picking his way through the bodies towards them.

'Over here,' Li replied, putting her hand up.

The steward hopped over a few pairs of outstretched legs and held out a piece of paper. 'Message for you. And by the way, congratulations.'

'Thanks,' they chorused.

Li opened the note. It was a printout of an e-mail. She read it out. "'I have just visited my daughter in hospital, where she is making good progress. I would very much like to meet the brave team who rescued her. This is an open invitation to them to join me for a few days at Teak Lodge, my small conservation reserve in the north-eastern corner of the Luangwa National Park, so that I can thank them in person. Sincerely, Joe Chandler.'"

Paulo's eyes lit up. 'Cool,' he said enthusiastically.

'That'll do nicely,' grinned Amber.

'Just as long as they have some nice soft beds!' said Paulo. 'I could sleep for a month.'

5
BIG GAME

A few days later John Middleton came down the steps of the hotel and folded his tall body into the back of the cab. He had business to get back to in New York, and Amber and the others were waving him off on his way to the airport.

'By the way,' he said, 'two sports equipment firms are interested in sponsoring Team Alpha Force in this year's Eco Challenge in Patagonia. It'd be right on your doorstep, Paulo.'

Paulo felt he should say something appreciative. But if he sounded too keen he might upset Amber. 'Patagonia's nice,' he said.

'What did you tell them?' Amber asked her uncle.

'I said you'd think about it, of course.' He pulled the door closed. 'Have fun at the game reserve and don't feed the lions.'

As the taxi pulled away, Amber folded her arms crossly. 'I said he wouldn't let this go. He's like one of those pushy parents who want to put their kids on the stage.'

Hex poked her in the ribs. 'I don't think anyone would want to put *you* on the stage.'

Amber gave him a steely look. 'Your parents clearly abandoned you to be brought up by computers in a darkened room.'

'Hey, guys,' said Paulo. He was looking towards the end of the drive. A dusty open-topped Jeep had pulled over to let John Middleton's taxi pass. 'Do you think this is Joe Chandler?'

As the Jeep came closer, they saw the driver was a powerfully built jet-black African. 'Not quite Tessa's colouring,' quipped Li.

Alex was looking at the steel bars that formed a skeleton roof on the Jeep. The underside of the vehicle was also reinforced. 'Interesting,' he said.

'The last time I saw accessories like that, they were on a Land Rover my dad had been driving around a minefield.'

'So how is Tessa?' Paulo asked the question but it was the first thing everybody had wanted to know. The introductions had been made and they were on their way, speeding along a dual carriageway with the breeze in their faces. Four of them sat in the back, with Alex in the front passenger seat.

Their driver was one of Joe Chandler's rangers, Patrick Nabwalya. He had the kind of rugged features that suggested a lifetime spent out of doors and made his age impossible to guess. The Jeep also looked well worn: the steering wheel was bent out of shape like a tin can that had been stood on.

'Tessa's much better and Joe's been able to bring her home,' said Patrick, 'but she'll be out of action for a while. The wound's infected and she's on massive doses of antibiotic. If you hadn't done what you did, she wouldn't be here at all.'

'She's a very brave girl,' said Paulo.

'Yeah,' said Amber beside him. 'After you told me

about her pulling her leg off that stake, I don't think I'll eat for a week.'

'She was in a lot of pain,' said Hex. 'To do that took real guts.'

The road became narrower as they left the town behind. The crash barriers disappeared and on either side was bush – a wide plain of waving grass the colour of sand, studded with thin teak trees and bulging baobabs. Mountains formed indigo shadows on the horizon.

'Sorry about this old truck, by the way,' said Patrick. 'The smart Range Rover's being used to ferry some guests to the airport.' He shifted into four-wheel drive. 'However, that means we can take the scenic route.' He swung the wheel and swerved off the road into the golden grass.

'Hey, good move,' grinned Amber from the back seat.

A cluster of baboons skittered up a baobab tree. One sat in the branches with its long fingers in its mouth as though wondering what to do next.

'So what do you do at Teak Lodge?' Li asked Patrick.

'We're part of a network of game reserves. Our bit's about forty kilometres across. We run safaris and tours for small family groups, and sometimes we have gap year volunteers helping out for a few weeks, but our real work is protecting the elephants. At one time the poachers nearly wiped them out so we tag them with radio markers to track them. Then we know if the numbers are falling.'

'How much poaching is there now?' said Li.

'They used to set up snares all over the place. Now they can get machine guns and ammo on the black market.'

'And mines?' said Alex. 'We seem to be carrying some heavy armouring here.'

'No, the poachers don't set mines. There are grenades all over the place, dating back to the troubles.'

'The rebel insurgences in the seventies and eighties?' said Alex.

'Right.' Patrick nodded. 'Most of the park has been cleared but if you come across a fenced-off area with red tags, don't go in.' He checked the compass on the dashboard and made an adjustment to their course. 'It's mainly safe, though.'

'What about all these man-eating animals?' said Amber.

'They're generally frightened of people and keep their distance. Partly we have the poachers to thank for that. When clients want to see the animals we take them to hides high up in the trees – so they can get close to the animals in safety. But Tessa said you looked like you really know what you're doing with these animals. What's your background?'

It was Alex who replied. 'Oh, this and that. Li and Paulo grew up working with a wide variety of animals; my dad's in security and Hex and Amber are into communications.'

'While we're here we'd love to help out if we can,' said Amber. 'See how it all works; make ourselves useful.'

'Definitely,' said Li. 'We like active holidays.'

Patrick nodded, smiling to himself. 'That's just like Tessa. She's never happier than when she's getting her hands dirty or training for races. Her mother died in the election riots in the eighties so

Tessa was kind of brought up by Joe and me and any other rangers who happened to be around. Right from when she was really small she's helped with the animals. Since Joe brought her home from hospital she's been going stir crazy because she can't do anything. We've just had a pool installed and she's really annoyed she can't use it.'

Patrick swerved around a deep rut in the ground, his hands gripping the kink in the steering wheel.

Amber pointed at it. 'What happened to that?' she asked.

'A matriarch elephant charged at Joe,' replied Patrick. 'He only just got away in time.'

Li whistled.

'Hey, you've got a flare pistol in the door,' said Amber. She recognized the telltale shape of the handle sticking out of the pocket. 'What's that for?'

'All sorts of things,' Patrick smiled. 'Scaring animals . . . but mainly it's in case someone gets stuck after dark. Both our vehicles carry them.'

A hundred metres ahead, the ground levelled out and a fence appeared. The Jeep headed along it until it reached the road, where there was a gateway. Two figures in dark green stepped out from behind the fence. Patrick slowed. One of the men carried an AK-47 in the crook of his arm. The other, a small wiry man with the build of a jockey, grinned at Patrick.

The five members of Alpha Force stiffened. 'Poachers?' said Alex quietly to Patrick.

'No, this is the checkpoint for entering the park,' he replied. 'That little guy there is Gaston – he's the other ranger at Teak Lodge.'

The warden waved them on as they drove through. Gaston smiled at them before climbing onto a quad bike parked on the other side of the checkpoint and roaring off into the dust.

'The guy at the checkpoint had a machine gun,' said Alex once they were clear of the gates. 'That's pretty serious protection. Are the poachers heavily armed?'

'Yes. They're shot if they get caught with ivory, so they'll stop at nothing. And just recently they've been getting even more daring. See that bullet hole down in the door beside Amber? That happened three weeks ago – I was out with Gaston and we must have scared them off. It came out of nowhere. We never even saw them.'

Amber leaned down. The hole was about as wide as her finger; she could see through it to the ground below.

Alex pulled their attention away from the door. 'Look at that.' He pointed in front of the Jeep.

A fully grown elephant moved out of the bush. It was enormous, a great grey mass, moving in slow motion.

'It's fantastic,' said Alex. His voice was an awestruck whisper. 'Look at the size of it.'

As if floating on air, ears flapping slowly like pterodactyl wings, the elephant came towards them, growing taller and taller. Patrick slowed.

'She's a mother, look,' whispered Amber. Two younger elephants sheltered under the great grey body.

'But she's got tusks,' said Hex.

'Matriarchs have tusks too,' said Patrick in a hushed voice. 'We've got to be very careful as she's got her babies with her. We'll stop and let her go past.' He halted the vehicle gently. 'No sudden movements. Everyone sit still.'

But the elephant walked right up to the Jeep and stopped in front of it. Her craggy face loomed over them, the tusks nearly as long as the vehicle's bonnet. Her eyes were like black sloes. It was like an immense statue in an ancient tomb coming to life.

The five members of Alpha Force looked to Patrick for a lead; he didn't move a muscle.

The elephant shattered the silence with a trumpet-burst through her trunk. The sound was ear-splitting. The six passengers sat transfixed by the awesome display of animal power.

Then she flicked her trunk at them and walked away, her youngsters trotting behind her.

Patrick spoke in a low voice as he put the Jeep in gear. 'That's Boudicca. She's been on the reserve for forty years. She just likes to warn us away from her family.'

6
TEAK LODGE

A man came down the steps, his hands tucked into the pockets of his dusty jeans. From the way he walked purposefully towards them, smiling in welcome, they guessed he must be Joe Chandler. He was older than any of Alpha Force had expected, well into his fifties, with a liberal sprinkling of grey through his thick head of hair. But he still had a powerful frame and moved with assurance, like an old cowboy.

Patrick halted the Jeep and cut the engine as Joe enthusiastically shook everyone's hand and introductions were made. 'Welcome to Teak Lodge,' he said. 'Make yourselves at home. Let me help with your luggage.'

Teak Lodge was a long, low wooden building lying along the crest of a hill. A veranda ran along its whole length, and two white pillars marked the entrance. The ground sloped gently away into a valley, mottled with grasses that varied in colour from grey-green to golden. Further away, clusters of animals moved slowly across the plains – the substantial dark blobs of buffalo, the stripy confusion of a herd of zebra.

'Say,' said Amber as she dragged her suitcase out of the back of the Jeep, 'you've got more visitors.'

A pair of giraffes stalked towards the far end of the building, their necks rocking gently with each leisurely stride.

'They come here all the time,' said Patrick.

Hex was amazed. The combination of wild animals and the smart, modern-looking house made his head spin. 'Don't you mind giraffes wandering around the garden?' he said.

'There isn't a garden,' said Joe, 'and the animals

don't understand boundaries. We have the check-points but they're to keep *people* in and out. The animals go where they want. Speaking of which, I'll show you to your rooms. Tessa's resting but she'll be down later.'

Li was also fascinated by the giraffes. 'They're so weirdly built but so graceful,' she said. 'Look at the way they move.' The animals continued their sedate promenade and went round the corner of the building.

'They're like aliens,' said Hex. 'They look like they're in low gravity.'

Amber dug him in the ribs. 'Poor Hex. Didn't you pack Safari Simulator for Nerds?'

Amber and Li were given a room together in the upstairs extension. As they were unpacking there was a knock at the door, then Alex popped his head round. 'Anyone coming for a swim? We can christen the new pool.'

'Wow, definitely!' Amber's face lit up. 'It'll do my ankle good. I must start using it now that it's more or less healed.'

Li looked sceptical. 'But isn't it starting to rain?'

'What, worried you'll get wet?' teased Alex.

'Anyway, swimming in the rain's fantastic,' said Amber.

'OK, we'll be down in five,' said Li.

Alex left them to get changed.

Li and Amber wasted no time in digging out swimwear. As they stripped off, Li noticed something silhouetted against the window.

She giggled. 'Amber, we've got a peeping tom – look.' She was looking behind Amber, out of the window.

Amber turned and saw a giraffe's head, silhouetted in three-quarter profile against the sky. The tips of its horns almost reached the top of the window. 'My God, how tall are those things?' She giggled as she shook out her dark red bikini bottoms. 'I hope it's female.'

The giraffe swayed out of view. Li stepped into her blue tie-dyed costume as Amber put on her bikini briefs and rummaged in her case for the top half.

'It's back – look!' squealed Li.

Amber looked round. The giraffe head glided back past the window again.

'It must like that bikini,' said Li.

Amber wriggled into her bikini top – a tight-fitting vest with crossover straps. Halfway, she got stuck. 'Li, can you give me a hand with this? It seems to have been designed for a contortionist.'

Li pulled up the straps of her swimsuit and went to help Amber.

The giraffe returned a third time, its head floating into view serenely. A voice boomed, 'Say cheese!' There was a flash like a camera going off. The giraffe capsized out of view like a tree falling.

Li and Amber shrieked and ran to the window. Hex and Paulo were below, staggering under a tall pole like a broom handle. On the end of it, they saw now, was a wooden cut-out head of a giraffe. Lashed to the pole was a length of plastic tube that ended just below the neck of the giraffe. The two boys were convulsed with laughter, which rather interfered with their efforts to make a clean getaway.

'I see you, Hex,' yelled Amber. 'You boys are so dead.'

Paulo gave up dismantling the creature and put his mouth to the plastic tube. His voice boomed out of the other end: 'Remember, girls, to keep your curtains closed in future.'

'Have you taken a picture of us?' shouted Li.

Paulo took his mouth away from the tube. 'Who knows?' He gave them his most enigmatic smile. 'Hex rigged that up.'

'Right,' said Li. 'This means war. At the swimming pool.' She ducked back into the room, snatched up a towel, crossed to the door, and was out in the corridor in a flash.

'Ow,' said Amber, hobbling after her. 'I can't run.'

Amber went slowly down the stairs, using the banisters as a crutch. But when she got to the bottom, Li was already outside, pursuing the boys into the pool. Amber heard big splashes and shrieks of delight. She cursed her ankle yet again. 'When I'm better,' she muttered, 'there'll be no stopping me.'

Someone was coming in from the pool, a slight figure lurching on a walking stick. She was visible only in silhouette, the pool an inviting bright rectangle of turquoise behind her. One of the girl's legs was slim, the other was enormous – twice the size. She walked painfully and slowly towards Amber.

'You must be the elusive Amber. I'm Tessa.' She held out her hand. 'It's irritating, this rain, isn't it? Now I've got to sit indoors because of my bandage; I'm not supposed to get it wet.'

Amber looked down and saw that the thicker leg was heavily bandaged, all the way down to the toes. Above the dressings it looked swollen, and yellowed with bruising. Amber shook Tessa's hand. 'I heard all about you from the others,' she said. 'That was some gruesome accident.'

'And I hear that you're lame too,' said Tessa, looking down at Amber's ankle. It looked almost back to normal, but Amber was still favouring it. Tessa let out a sigh and tucked a blonde curl behind her ear. 'Frustrating, isn't it?'

'Absolutely,' agreed Amber. 'I had to sit out the whole race. I didn't know what to do with myself.'

'All I can do is sit,' said Tessa, her face screwed up. 'I've never sat still in my life. The last few years, I've been training the whole time. Whatever the weather, I train. Now I have to stay in if there's a drop of rain.' She paused. 'Sorry, that was a bit of a rant. You were on your way to swim. You don't want to listen to me.'

'Believe me, I know how you feel.' Amber laughed good naturedly. Tessa's frustration brought back her own all too clearly. 'I did sit-ups and press-ups while the others were racing.'

Tessa's face broke out in a big smile. 'Oh, it's so long since I had a good conversation about working out. I want to hear all about what you guys do to train. I've got withdrawal symptoms.' Her expression suddenly changed. She was tanned but her skin was pale and clammy. She looked as though she might pass out.

Amber caught her arm. 'Are you OK?'

Tessa nodded and tried to pull away, but another wave of giddiness came over her. 'I think I just need to lie down,' she said. She spoke through clamped teeth as though she was fighting the urge to be sick.

'Can I do anything?' said Amber. 'Should I get your father or call a doctor?'

Tessa shook her head. 'It's the antibiotics. You

should see how many I'm taking – enough for an elephant.'

'At least let me see you to your room,' said Amber.

'Oh, I'll be OK in the lounge,' said Tessa. 'Besides, I've got to put that away before my dad sees it.' She nodded towards the reception area. Lying along the counter was a long pole with a giraffe's head attached to it.

Amber went over and picked it up. It had originally been painted with a lifelike portrait of a giraffe, but the paint was peeling and old. It was funny to think how convincing it had looked in silhouette. Amber turned it over and had a quick look for signs of the promised camera, but of course there was nothing.

'It's hideous, isn't it?' said Tessa. 'I used to have it in my room when I was little. It was the old sign in the bar – it used to be called the Rubbernecks Bar when we first came here. There's a load of old stuff lying around that belonged to the previous owners. Some of it was really gross – like leopard skins and stuffed heads. In those days people used to come here to actually shoot animals.'

Amber put the sign back down on the counter. 'The boys had this earlier. How on earth did they get hold of it?'

Tessa grinned. 'I left it propped up outside their room as a giggle. It was in the window. I listened outside the door. It took them a good few minutes to work out it wasn't a real giraffe standing there – they were so funny.'

Amber smiled to herself. Outside, she could hear shrieks and shouts as Li dispensed wet justice to the boys. She picked up the sign again. 'Where do you want this?'

'Tessa says you are confident and knowledgeable around animals,' said Joe Chandler.

They were all in the lounge sitting around a large table, with Patrick and Gaston. They had eaten superb steaks, barbecued by Joe, and were now exploring a map of the lodge and surrounding area.

Tessa was on a large sofa, her bad leg propped up by cushions. 'They can come with us when we go out tomorrow morning on patrol,' she said. She sounded enthusiastic, but Amber caught that same tone in her voice that she had heard earlier – as though she was forcing herself to go on when she was very tired.

Before Amber could say anything, Joe was up and at Tessa's side. 'Are you all right, Tess?' he said. He put his hand to her forehead. Tessa protested, but only weakly. Joe stepped back. 'I think you're running a temperature. You ought to be in bed.'

'Oh no,' said Tessa. 'I'm just a bit tired.'

'You've been overdoing it,' said Joe. 'Come on, let's get you upstairs.' He took her gently by the elbow.

'I'm underdoing it, that's the problem,' muttered Tessa. But she allowed Joe to walk her to the door. Just before they reached it she turned round. 'Sorry, you guys,' she said to Alpha Force. 'But we'll be up bright and early tomorrow to do a patrol, OK?'

'OK,' agreed Paulo and Hex. 'Goodnight, Tessa.'

'Sleep tight,' said Alex.

'Take it easy,' added Amber.

'See you in the morning,' said Li.

Patrick's face was etched with concern as he watched them go down the corridor.

'Is she all right?' said Paulo. 'She looks quite ill.'

Patrick shrugged. 'The doctors said the drugs would make her feel bad but she should be all right. We just need to keep an eye on her. And Joe's right, she doesn't know the meaning of rest.'

Gaston nodded slowly, his compact features earnest. 'Before she did the race she used to train by running alongside me in the Jeep for the whole morning.'

'Wow,' said Alex. 'That's a pretty good workout.'

'She's just like her mother was,' said Gaston. 'She used to run marathons all the time.'

Patrick smiled. 'Full of energy, that's our Tessa. She wants to change the world, stamp out animal poaching and be a champion long-distance runner. This injury has been a big blow. She had a lot of competitions lined up.'

'Still, enough of such gloomy talk,' said Gaston. 'We're monitoring the elephants tomorrow, so you can tag along for the ride if you want. Or do you want to see some lions?'

Li and Paulo had the same thought going through their heads. Having had to avoid the lions during the race crisis, they were itching to study them at closer quarters. 'Lions,' they said together.

At almost the same moment Alex, Hex and Amber were thinking of the immense creature they'd seen at the gates. 'Elephants,' they chorused.

'Actually, both,' said Li.

'I think we can arrange that,' grinned Patrick.

7
LIONS

Joe's face looked drawn as he came down the stairs into the foyer the next morning. The sun wasn't yet up but Alpha Force were ready to go. Dawn was the best time to see the animals; it was when they visited the water holes or went hunting.

'Tessa's not coming down,' Joe told them. 'She's got a temperature so I've made her stay in bed. If she's no better by lunch time I'm going to call the doctor. She's really disappointed because she was looking forward to coming with you. She made me promise to let you come up and tell her about it when you're back.'

'Absolutely,' said Amber.

Outside on the veranda, they saw the Range Rover pulling up. The handbrake rasped. Patrick leaned out of the window. 'Who's for the lions?'

'That's us,' said Paulo, taking Li by the arm.

'See you later, guys,' said Li. 'Enjoy the elephants.'

Patrick drove them down the slope and out onto the plain. He slowed for a moment, his head cocked and listening. As the engine noise quietened he asked, 'Did you hear that?'

A roar sounded from the black sky. It was loud and long. Paulo caught Li's eye. 'Yes,' he said, 'and I feel a lot better than I did the last time I heard it.'

Patrick drove on for about ten minutes. From time to time, roars rumbled across the plain. Each time they heard them, Patrick would stop and listen, and check he was still heading in the right direction. Although they were safe in the Range Rover, it was still an eerie sound in the pre-dawn darkness.

'I think they're here,' said Patrick and halted again. He cut the engine, turned off the headlights and switched on a torch. As he swung it around, an acacia bush sprang into view, and with it the reflections of fifteen pairs of eyes.

Li and Paulo gasped softly. Lions. A whole family of them.

Patrick looked pleased at their reaction. 'OK, it's the same drill as it was with the elephant: no sudden movements. They're a safe distance away and we're going to get out and climb up into that hide there.' He flashed the torch in the direction of a tree. Metal struts had been hammered into the trunk to make a ladder. 'We should be safe because they're used to seeing people do this, and because they've got a kill. You know you should never under any circumstances attempt to feed a lion or put food out for them?'

Li nodded. 'It makes them lose their fear of humans.'

Patrick smiled. 'That's right. But you'd be amazed at the number of people who want to do it.' He got out of the Range Rover and shone the torch at the ladder. 'Li, you go up first.'

They climbed up. At the top, eight metres up the tree, was a hide like a tree house, with wooden benches and a thatched roof. A long slitted window ran horizontally all the way round, like in a pillbox, giving a 360-degree view of the plain.

The sun started to light the horizon; the sky was turning pale.

The lions were feeding on a zebra. They gave the visitors a moment's attention and returned to their meal, pulling at the flesh with their teeth. After they had stripped off the meat they licked the shafts of the long bones clean, purring as they worked.

From the hide the three watchers could smell the carcass; even at that distance it was strong and meaty. Paulo shuddered. 'That was nearly us,' he said to Li in a low voice.

'Makes you think, doesn't it?' said Li.

Patrick hadn't heard them. 'All the prides have names,' he said. 'This is Red Pride's territory. It has ten lionesses.'

'That makes it very strong,' said Li.

'You obviously know about lions, Li,' said Patrick. 'Have you worked with them?'

'My parents are zoologists. They did some research

at the Lion Study Center in Minnesota a few years back.'

'Fascinating,' said Patrick. 'What was the project?'

'To find out whether lionesses preferred lions with light manes or dark ones.'

'And what was the answer?' said Paulo. 'Tall, dark and handsome?'

'No idea. I expect they spent the whole time wondering how to ask them.' She gave him a withering smile.

Paulo had a pair of binoculars around his neck. Now that it was light enough to use them, he put them to his eyes and focused. 'Do you monitor the lions as well as the elephants?' He handed the binoculars to Li.

Patrick shook his head. 'The lions are monitored by a separate reserve. But they make their own territories and roam all over. Which is good for when we have clients on safari.'

'Like giraffes,' said Li. She gave Paulo a pointed look before taking the binoculars and lifting them to her eyes.

'It's amazing what you can see when you're a giraffe,' replied Paulo with a twinkling smile. 'I can't wait for that film to be developed.' He gasped. 'Hey, look.'

Li was about to tell him sternly not to change the subject, but when she lowered the binoculars all such thoughts vanished from her head. Five cubs, overcome with curiosity, had sauntered over to investigate the Range Rover. They sniffed the tyres and bumpers, licking them and pulling faces. Two of them stood on their hind legs and tried to look into the vehicle. When they got down they left big paw prints in the dust on the bodywork. The other three started playing tag around the wheels.

'Wow,' breathed Paulo.

As the sun came up, the pride moved away from their meal to find a shady spot and stretched out for a sleep. Vultures immediately swooped on the remains and the carcass disappeared under their scrawny, feathered bodies.

'We can go down now,' said Patrick. 'They're far enough away.' He clambered out of the tree house.

'I'll go first,' said Li to Paulo, 'in case you've got another hidden camera.' She turned to step backwards off the platform. The rung had condensation on it from the morning dew and her foot slipped.

Paulo was having a last look through the binoculars. When he lowered them and turned round, he expected to see Li disappearing down the ladder. But she was still in the doorway, rooted to the spot. Her fingers clung to the wooden door-surround and her sleeveless top showed the muscles in her shoulders, rigid like ropes under tension. She had one foot still on the sill of the entrance, the other on the top rung.

'Li?' he said. 'Is there another lion down there?'

She shook her head. She couldn't speak.

Then Paulo remembered her reaction on the cliff face. Li had frozen then too. He hadn't thought any more about it until now; there were many odd, once-in-a-lifetime things that had happened because the team were exhausted. Like falling asleep while riding a bicycle. But for Li to freeze here and now was different.

Paulo moved cautiously towards her.

Her eyes widened, warning him not to come near. 'Don't,' she said. Her voice was harsh. Her pupils dilated so far they made her eyes look like hollow black circles.

Paulo's mind raced. What was going on? 'Li,' he asked gently, 'what do you want me to do? Shall I help you down?'

Her expression said *Keep away*, but a tear rolled out of one eye. She nodded.

'Can you give me your hand? I'll come and lie on the floor and hold onto you as you get onto the ladder. I won't let go until you're safely climbing down.' He walked carefully to the doorway, kneeled down in front of her and held out his hand.

She grabbed it as though she was grabbing a lifeline. Her grip was crushing. Bracing herself on the door frame, she lowered her foot carefully to the second rung. Her nails dug into Paulo's hand.

'It's OK, Li, I've got you,' he said. 'I'll keep holding until you say. And I promise there are no giraffes with cameras.'

She smiled, but it looked like a rictus of fear; it didn't make her relax. She stepped down onto the next rung. Paulo could feel her shaking. Something had transformed Li, the bravest, most talented climber he knew, into this nervous wreck. What had happened and when? Was it the abseil event?

Bit by bit, he lowered her down until she had both hands and feet on the ladder. She suddenly climbed down very fast, her face tight with concentration, until her feet touched firm ground – then he saw the tension drain out of her face. But it was replaced by anger. Again, Paulo remembered the cliff face. She had climbed down quickly and was furious afterwards, as if punishing herself.

He pattered quickly down the ladder. Should he say something?

Patrick was already in the Range Rover, the engine running.

Li touched Paulo on the arm. 'Don't say anything to the others,' she said. Her eyes were pleading. 'Promise?'

Paulo nodded gravely. 'I promise.'

8
INTRUDERS

Joe Chandler drove through the bush with Hex, Alex and Amber. It was dawn; the sky was turning grey and would soon be light.

'We check at least one of the watering holes every morning at about this time,' he said. 'It's the best way to find out if any new elephants have come into the area. They're always on the move; the ones we've tagged wander off to other areas of the park, onto the patch of another reserve, and elephants from other reserves wander into our area. But there are always some who haven't been tagged at all, so that's what we're looking for now.'

In the passenger seat, Hex carried a radio receiver with an antenna. In the back, Alex and Amber peered over his shoulder at the display. A red light winked, showing that tagged elephants were nearby. Hex tried pointing it in a different direction to see if the beeps came any faster, but they didn't. It didn't seem to be very sensitive. In his head he was already making modifications.

'When you get very close to an elephant we've tagged,' said Joe Chandler, 'the needle goes into the red.'

'Ah, I see,' said Hex. 'A simple ammeter. Does each elephant have its own code?'

Joe nodded. 'Yes, the machine automatically logs the one we've seen. Then we download it into the computer back at the lodge.'

Colour began to blush into the sky with the dawn. The grey shapes of trees around them started to look green. A flock of guinea-fowl rose as the Jeep passed them, making a plaintive noise. Shapes started to move through the grasses: gazelle, puku and waterbuck.

'Elephant ahoy,' said Amber.

Hex looked at the dial. 'No there isn't.'

'Not on your Gameboy,' said Amber. 'In real life.'

In the clearing, about thirty metres away, a small family of three elephants was walking out of the forest, heading for a river.

'Good,' said Joe. 'These must be ones that haven't been tagged.' He lowered his voice to a whisper even though the animals were still some way off.

'Which one's the matriarch?' said Amber.

'That one at the front. Look, she's checking for danger.'

The large female elephant lifted her trunk above her head and swivelled it like a periscope, one foot raised in mid stride.

Joe stopped the Jeep and cut the engine, then got out. 'I've got my darting gun so we can tag them now—'

He got no further. The matriarch swung her huge bulk round. The other elephants turned with her and hurried back into the wood, flapping their ears wildly.

Joe hadn't even got the tranquillizer gun out of

the back of the Jeep. He shrugged and walked back to the driver's door.

'Did we scare them off?' said Amber.

Joe pulled the door open. 'Yes and no. The poachers have made some of them so scared of people, they won't even go to the water for a drink. We'll have to come back later and track them from here. They'll be less nervy in the heat of the day.'

'Oh my God,' said Alex quietly. 'I don't think it was us. Look.' His mouth was tight with shock.

'Get out with your hands up.' The voice was deep. Its African accent carried a note of menace.

Three figures stood beside the Jeep with AK-47 assault rifles. Ammo belts criss-crossed their chests and glinted in the morning sun. One of the men was black; he had a scar on his cheek, as though a piece of the flesh had been gouged out with a chisel. The other two were white – one with a dirty yellow bandanna; the other with an animal tooth set in silver on a chain around his neck.

The man in the bandanna talked to the two others. The words sounded urgent and harsh. Amber recognized it as similar to French; but they were speaking too fast for her to make out the words.

Amber glanced at Joe's face. It was set and grim. When she saw that, she didn't need vocabulary: the intention behind the words was clear. They were probably discussing how to kill them.

The scarred man spoke in English again and jerked the end of his weapon. 'Out.'

Joe Chandler put his hands up in the international gesture of submission and stepped away from the Jeep. Hex followed his lead. He put the tracking device down on the floor and stepped carefully out. Alex, in the back, put his leg over the side of the Jeep and slid to the ground. He raised his hands carefully.

'And her,' said the man with the animal tooth. A hyena's. It wouldn't have looked out of place in his narrow, snout-like mouth, thought Amber.

Alex glanced at Amber. She was climbing carefully out of the Jeep, lying on her front and swivelling herself round awkwardly. Her ankle must still be quite sore, thought Alex. 'Give her a moment,' he said to the poachers. 'She's injured.'

The scarred man and the man in the yellow bandanna stepped forwards, intending to grab Amber and hurry her along. Amber whirled round. In her hand was the Jeep's spare petrol can. She hurled its contents at the poachers. Petrol splashed all over them.

Scarface and Yellow Bandanna leaped back, but dark stains were spreading over their green fatigues. The fumes caught the back of Amber's throat – a rich smell of pure danger. Yellow Bandanna shot off a barrage of angry words, but in his eyes she could see his fear.

Hyena-tooth, who had been out of range, grabbed Alex by the arm and pressed the muzzle of the gun into his belly. 'Stay where you are,' he said roughly.

'No, you stay where you are,' retorted Amber. In her hands was the flare pistol.

She brought it up and levelled it at the two petrol-soaked figures in front of her. 'If you don't let us go I'm going to fire, and you two are going up in flames. So you're going to stay nice and still while we all get back in our vehicle and go on our way. And don't even think of getting up to any funny business, like shooting at us as we leave. These guns have quite a range.'

Scarface barked something at the man holding Alex. Alex was released. He backed away.

Joe Chandler and Hex lowered their hands and stepped slowly back towards the Jeep. Joe's hand shook for a moment as he reached for the driver's door, but then he steadied it and got in. He was a tough guy but this had shocked him.

Hex climbed into the passenger seat. Amber hopped into the back, keeping her attention fixed on the poachers.

The man with the scar spat some words at her in his rough language. Amber gave him some back in plain English.

Joe gunned the engine and they sped away.

Amber leaned out of the back. Making a support out of her elbows, she kept the flare gun trained on the poachers. Just you try going for a weapon, her feral smile said, and I'll fire. They glowered at her, their faces tight with rage.

Joe hammered the Jeep at full speed. At last

Amber decided they were far enough away to be out of range of their machine guns. She turned round and handed the flare gun back to Alex. 'Patrick was right. These do have all sorts of uses.'

Joe was looking at a far point on the horizon. 'I really thought we'd had it then. I've never got that close to them. Amber, you were brilliant.'

'I would have thought they'd stay out of sight,' said Hex. 'Surely they don't want to be caught.'

'Yes, they normally keep well away from us,' said Joe. 'That is, until recently. Lately they've been getting a lot more aggressive. They must have wanted us out of the way so they could pursue those elephants, and they weren't prepared to wait till we left of our own accord. We've got three guests coming this morning. I hope there's no trouble when we take them out.' He sighed; a long, drawn-out sound as though he was trying to bring his pounding heart back to normal. Then he looked at his three passengers. 'Now you've saved my life as well as Tessa's.'

9
FEAR

Something was really wrong with Li, decided Paulo. As they travelled back with Patrick, she talked about the lions, bombarding the ranger with questions. Paulo couldn't get a word in. But he didn't want to – he was too worried about Li. She was talking nineteen to the dozen, as if to stop anyone thinking about what had happened on the ladder. Patrick must have seen Paulo lower her down. Was she scared he might ask about it? Or was she more scared that he, Paulo, might?

Patrick drove the Range Rover up to the front

door and braked. 'I'll drop you guys here. I've got to go and see to something in the workshop.'

Li jumped out. Paulo followed. 'Thanks, Patrick,' he said. 'The lions were great.'

'Yeah, thanks,' said Li. 'See you later.'

At one of the upstairs windows, a curtain twitched. 'Is that Tessa's room?' asked Li. 'She'll want to hear about it. Let's go and keep her company.' She strode into the lodge, energetic as always when she had a purpose.

Paulo's eyes narrowed. Was that purpose to run away from him? He caught up with her in the foyer. 'Li,' he said. His eyes were earnest. 'We've got to talk.'

Li stopped. When she replied she was biting her lip. 'Later. Maybe.' She started to move off again.

Paulo skipped in front of her, blocking her way. 'No, Li. It has to be now. What happened out there wasn't just a one-off; it happened in the race and I think it's happened before then, too.'

She looked away from him, as though she couldn't face his searching eyes.

Paulo had to choose his words very carefully. It

would be so easy to put too much pressure on her and scare her into denying anything was wrong. But he couldn't let her go on bottling up a problem like this. He put a hand on her arm and squeezed it reassuringly. 'I don't mean to be harsh. But this isn't just your problem. What if my life depended on your skills? Or Alex's life, or Amber's, or Hex's?'

Li stared past him for a moment, then nodded.

She wanted to go somewhere utterly private. Amber was due back soon, so their room wouldn't do. The same went for the boys' room. So they made their way to the other guest wing and found an empty room that was open for airing.

Paulo sat on the bare mattress. Li sat in an armchair, but perched tensely on the edge, her head in her hands.

'It was just before we all came out to do the race. You know my folks are in England at the moment?' She spoke in a low voice, as though she was afraid that even this far away from anyone else, she might be overheard. 'We were in Derbyshire and there's a lot of climbing around there. It's all rugged peaks and rocky outcrops. I fancied the idea of getting some practice so I called Dina, my old climbing instructor. She'd got a summer job at a teaching centre. Anyway, we'd climbed a thirty-foot slab – you know, that's jargon for a sheer cliff – and were going to ab back down.'

'Ab?' repeated Paulo.

'Abseil. Anyway, Dina went first. I gave her a bit of time to get down. Then I heard a scream.

'I thought at first she was messing about. I was actually about to tell her to can it. But I looked over the edge instead. She was at the bottom of the cliff. There was a great jagged rock and she had fallen across it. Her back literally snapped over it; it looked like an upside-down V.'

Paulo was shocked, but he kept it to himself. It was hard enough for Li to tell him this. If he interrupted it might distract her.

Li's voice sank to a whisper. 'That wasn't the worst thing. She was still conscious. I shouted to her not to move, but she sort of wriggled. When she did, she screamed in agony. I've not been able to forget it – I don't think I ever will. It was like nothing I've ever heard before. When she fell off the rock and screamed it was sort of unreal, you know? Almost ethereal. But this . . . I've heard it again and again in my head. Find some way of plugging my brain into a tape recorder and you'll know what I mean.'

Li let out a ragged sigh and continued. 'She screamed for ages. Gradually the sounds got weaker and weaker. Finally the medics arrived and gave her an injection. She passed out immediately. I was still at the top of the slab, in my harness. I wanted to go to her but I couldn't move. I felt sick. I tried to check my gear. But all the knots and clips looked like spaghetti. I knew I should look for a prussik knot – never mind what that is, it's just a knot – but it was like my brain had crashed and refused to reboot. It was like being asked a question in an exam, and having no idea what it even means.

'I waited there for ages. Finally one of the rangers got me down. That was really embarrassing. They thought I was some silly girl who'd bitten off more than I could chew.

'There was an inquiry. All Dina's equipment was fine, correctly put together. Of course it was – she's a pro. But the rope had snapped. She did everything right but now she's quadriplegic. I used to just think, Hey, accidents happen, that's part of climbing. If you're careful you'll be OK. But Dina *was* careful. She just had a bit of bad luck. And I was borrowing her equipment, so it was luck that gave *her* the bad rope and not me.'

Li ran her fingers through her silky hair and dug them into her scalp. 'But I don't know why I keep thinking like that. With Alpha Force I've seen so many things. I've seen people injured horribly, I've escaped death more times than I can count. Do you remember when you got me out of that minefield?'

Paulo nodded.

'I didn't go to pieces after that. But I saw Dina fall off a rock face, doing something that ordinary members of the public do, and I'm a nervous wreck.'

Paulo doubted that most ordinary members of the public climbed the kind of peaks Li did, but he kept that to himself. He said gently, 'She's a friend; no wonder you're affected by it. And perhaps all these other things are catching up with you.'

'They're not catching up with me,' Li retorted

hotly. 'I've barely got started yet. I'll do anything you like – walk into another minefield to get my friends out of danger. I haven't lost my nerve.'

'Li, you don't have to prove anything. Just take your time. You'll be all right. Your confidence will return.'

Li snorted. 'How? I climb a tree and I need the fire brigade to help me down! What earthly use am I to Alpha Force like that?'

Paulo gave her a wry grin. 'I'll rescue you. I always wanted to be a fireman.' But his brain was reeling from the horrible story Li had told him. He became serious. 'Listen, Li, you'll get through this. We're all going to get bad patches from time to time. It's a tough life we've chosen. But remember the race? We helped each other through. Alpha Force is about teamwork.'

Li was silent. Then she said, 'You can't tell the others. Not yet. Promise you won't.'

He nodded, but he wished he didn't feel so help-less. 'We'd better get back,' he said. 'They'll be wondering where we are.'

'You're right,' agreed Li.

Paulo watched her as she stood up and moved to the door; she seemed a little more relaxed, less edgy. Talking had done her good. Maybe that would be all she needed; maybe now she could leave the fear behind.

Someone opened the door before Li had even touched the handle. A voice boomed in: 'Aha, caught you!'

Paulo jumped to his feet, shocked. Outside in the dark corridor, Tessa was grinning back at them, her hand on the door handle. Li and Paulo glanced at each other. They were both thinking the same thing: had she heard?

'I knew there was something between you two,' said Tessa, wagging her finger as her smile spread wider. She was breathing hard, as though she had just been running. 'You're looking all guilty. Sneaking off for a quick tryst, eh?'

Li was about to agree for the sake of keeping her secret, but then Tessa's expression changed. Her smile faded. She shivered and leaned more heavily on the door handle.

'Actually, guys,' she said, 'I don't feel at all good. Have you seen my dad?'

Paulo dived to catch her as she tumbled to the floor. 'Quick, Li,' he said. 'Call an ambulance.'

The ambulance was there when Joe Chandler got back with Amber, Alex and Hex. Hex glanced across at Joe and caught the look of panic on his face as he braked, cut the engine and jumped out of the Jeep.

Li and Patrick ran out of the door to meet him.

'Tessa's gone into septic shock,' said Li breathlessly. 'The infection from the wound has got into her bloodstream. They're going to have to take her to hospital.'

Behind her, the paramedics pushed Tessa down the front steps on a trolley. She lay wrapped in a red blanket, a drip plumbed into her hand and connected to a bag of clear liquid that rested on her chest. Paulo was with her. He held onto the bag of liquid to stop it falling as the trolley clattered onto the grass.

Joe looked from his daughter's face to the face of the paramedic in front of him. 'Will she be all right?'

'She's very ill,' replied the paramedic. His colleague jumped into the ambulance and pulled the trolley in. 'You'd better come with us.'

Joe's eyes met Patrick's in an unspoken question. 'Go,' said Patrick. 'We can manage here.'

Joe climbed into the back of the ambulance. A paramedic pulled the doors closed and the ambulance sped off.

Alex, Hex and Amber were still in the Jeep. 'I thought she was on antibiotics,' said Amber.

'They weren't enough,' said Paulo.

10
MOYA

'We found this calf about a week ago. Poachers had killed her mother and she was in a bad way.'

They had just had breakfast, and Patrick had led them round to the yard behind the lodge. It was a wide, sandy area with two large pens marked out by ranch-style fencing. A baby elephant stood in the corner of one, watching them with dark eyes. It was time to feed her.

Amber thought she was about the cutest thing she had ever seen, a perfect, petite version of the mighty Boudicca who had met them at the gate. She wanted to say something gushing but she restrained herself; she'd never live it down. Instead she went for something eminently sensible: 'She looks rather unhappy.'

Patrick nodded. 'She's ill. We found her the same day as Tessa had her accident. We told Tess about her when she was in hospital, and she insisted on naming her. She's called Moya.' As he spoke he fitted a large teat to a bottle of formula milk.

Still watching them, the baby elephant curled the end of her trunk into her mouth and sucked it.

Unlike Amber, Paulo had no inhibitions about responding to the creature. He leaned over the fence and caught Moya's eye, giving her a great, welcoming grin.

Moya knew a friendly face when she saw one. She trotted up to him eagerly, her ears forward, framing her face like butterfly wings.

Paulo put his hand down and stroked Moya's head. The baby elephant twisted her head round and tried to get his fingers in her mouth.

Hex flinched backwards on Paulo's behalf. 'Careful, Paulo. Patrick, does she bite?'

It was Paulo who answered. 'She just wants some

milk.' He offered Moya his thumb, just as he used to with the calves on his ranch. The elephant pulled it into her mouth, making sucking noises. Paulo looked round at the others, enchanted. 'Her tongue's really soft.'

'Ladies and gentlemen,' said Li, 'I give you Paulo, the man who suckles elephants.'

Patrick was ready with the milk bottle. Moya saw it and tried to reach for it with her trunk, but missed and clouted Paulo on the side of the head.

Paulo reeled backwards, his head ringing. Even though the elephant was only small, it was like being lashed with a thick cable. 'Ouch, I just saw stars then.' He shook his head.

'Careful, Paulo,' said Patrick. 'That's happened to me and it really hurts. She doesn't have much co-ordination yet; she has to learn how to use her trunk. But a fully grown elephant could cave your skull in with a blow like that.'

Moya had leaped backwards as Paulo yelped and now stood eyeing him nervously, her trunk looped into her mouth again. Patrick leaned over the fence and tried to coax her over to him.

'Patrick,' said Paulo, 'may I feed her? I want to be friends with her.'

Patrick handed him the bottle. 'Be my guest. It may take you a while, though.'

Paulo followed his gaze to a crate on the ground. It held another seven bottles. He smiled. 'No problem.' He held out the teat to Moya. 'Come on, *querida*, time for breakfast.'

Li looked at Patrick. 'Did the poachers hurt her?'

'No, not physically; but they took away her mother. She didn't get enough antibodies from her mother's milk and now she's got an intestinal infection. Do you see how she's bloated around the tummy but thin everywhere else? She's not absorbing any food. We're giving her massive doses of antibiotics in the milk, but it doesn't seem to be helping much. She's always ravenous and she's getting thinner. I suggested that we shouldn't tell Tessa about her – we could have farmed her out to one of the other reserves – but Joe wanted to give her an incentive to get better. Anyway, now Tessa is probably too ill to remember she's here.'

Amber was aghast. 'You're not going to give up on Moya, are you?'

'Just tell us what to do and we'll nurse her,' said Li. 'Twenty-four/seven.'

Patrick shook his head slowly. 'It's not a question of that; we're doing all that can be done. We just have to hope that it works.'

Amber again voiced what they were all thinking. 'How bad *is* Tessa?'

Patrick took a deep breath. 'I've known people die of septic shock. It's bad.'

The baby elephant took a cautious step towards Paulo. Her lips opened and she let go of her trunk, which tumbled to the ground like a heavy rope. With the next step she took she trod on it and let out a shriek of surprised pain.

As one, Alpha Force dissolved in helpless laughter. After the shocking events of the past few hours it felt good to have something to laugh about.

Paulo leaned over the fence, coaxing her to come near. Hunger eventually overcame Moya's distrust. She sidled up to him, holding her trunk out of the way of her feet like a dowager lifting her skirts, and clamped her mouth onto the offered bottle. Once she had the teat she sucked ferociously. The milk bubbled and sloshed as she pulled on it. But now Patrick had pointed it out, Paulo saw that she did look unwell. The bones of her hips and shoulders were like razor blades under her rough hide, while her belly was swollen like a famine victim's.

'Hey,' said Alex, 'we've got company.'

Two adult elephants were ambling across the yard.

Patrick looked up. 'Oh, I thought it was about time for those two. That's Penelope, nearest to us; the guy next to her is her twelve-year-old son, Brains. There's another member of the family – Thunderbird – she should be around somewhere. We actually called her Thunderbird Two because when we found her, she had flattened a line of trees in a long avenue.' He grimaced. 'I guess you can tell Joe named these ones, not Tessa.'

Alex was astounded. No-one had heard the elephants arrive, yet they were more than three metres tall, with legs as stout as the pillars that held up the front of the lodge. Each elephant's head was as big as an entire zebra. 'How did they get past without us hearing?' he said. 'Look at the size of them.'

Patrick nodded. 'They can move silently when they want to. Elephants are amazing animals.'

The two elephants were clearly on a mission. They headed for a wooden outhouse, where there was a tap. Penelope lifted her trunk. At the end were two finger-like lips, which she lowered delicately onto the handle. Brains put his trunk over the nozzle of the tap, like a hose, while Penelope turned it on. A few drops fell onto the sandy earth, but most of it went up Brains's trunk.

'Did you teach them to do that?' said Hex.

'No,' said Patrick. 'One day we just found them doing it. They must have seen us. They're very intelligent.'

Brains took his trunk away from the tap, opened his mouth and squirted the water into it. Its upturned corners made him look as though he was laughing. Then he and Penelope reversed roles: Brains turned the tap on and Penelope took a drink.

'Are they tame?' said Li.

'Not tame as such,' said Patrick. 'I'd say they were friendly; they're used to us. They came one day because we had another orphaned calf here – that was Thunderbird. Now they've made this their watering hole. It's safer than the ones out in the park because they're not vulnerable to poachers.'

'I can't see any tags on them,' said Li.

'They're under the skin, in the neck,' Patrick explained.

'This must be Thunderbird,' said Alex.

Another elephant was trotting towards Brains and Penelope, her ears held out. She made a loud rumbling noise and the other two elephants turned away from the tap to greet her. As she reached them, they all twisted their trunks together, clacking their tusks like drumsticks and flapping their ears.

'Look,' said Li, 'Paulo's getting on well.' Moya gave a loud sigh and milk spurted down her chin and all over Paulo. It was the latest of many accidents. His dark-blue T-shirt and jeans were already soaking.

'I think he's in his element,' said Amber. 'Patrick, what will happen to Moya?'

'If she survives, we'll rehabilitate her into the wild. These three will probably get to know her and adopt her. We had Thunderbird here ten years ago and Penelope took her on. Before we started doing this, orphans went to zoos and circuses.'

Amber looked at Moya's thin shoulders. 'Was Thunderbird as bad as Moya?'

Patrick shook his head. 'No. I think Moya is worse.'

Paulo started Moya on the last bottle. She attempted to explore his face with the prehensile fingers on the end of her trunk. 'Hey,' he said gently, dodging a clumsy probe, 'you don't get me with that again.'

Thunderbird turned away from the group and they saw her other side for the first time. In the thin membrane of her ear were two bullet holes, like a punch made with a machine.

'Is that an old wound?' asked Hex.

'No,' said Patrick. His mouth was a tight line and his voice quivered with fury. 'I haven't seen that before. Some poacher's had a go at her.'

11

RANGERS

'Anyone know what this is?' Gaston laid the gun down on the bonnet of the Jeep with a wiry hand. Alpha Force were to go into the field with him. They were going to have another look for the unmarked elephants they had seen earlier and tranquillize them so that they could be tagged. They hoped the poachers hadn't got to them first.

Alex recognized most of the weapon's features. He pointed to each one as he reeled them off: 'Benjamin Sheridan stock, optional pistol grip, bolt action, point-five calibre smooth bore, two times pistol scope . . .'

Li put her finger on the long canister of propellant gas fixed to the underside of the barrel. 'It's a tranquillizer gun.'

'Have you ever used one?' asked Gaston.

Li shook her head. 'I haven't but my parents have. I've seen just enough to know that tranquillizer darts can be just as dangerous as bullets.'

Gaston nodded. 'That's all you need to know for now.' He took the tranquillizer gun and put it in the back of the Jeep. 'Hex, have you got the tracking unit?'

'All set,' Hex replied.

'Good afternoon,' called Patrick on his way past. He was leading three teenage boys to the Teak Lodge Range Rover. They looked Amber and Li up and down appreciatively as they walked past. Amber looked back, sizing up their expensively cut clothes. They positively bristled with designer labels.

One of the boys was talking to Patrick. He had wavy black hair and wore a crisply ironed shirt. 'So do we get to shoot?' he asked, trying to catch Amber's eye.

'Only with a camera,' said Patrick. Amber smirked. She could hear the patience in Patrick's voice was already strained.

The boy was showing off: 'My dad went on safari in Kenya and he was allowed to shoot a leopard with a tranquillizer gun. He got so close he was able to put his foot on it. My mum took a photo.'

'Some safari companies do that but we don't,' replied Patrick. 'This park is all about conservation. We don't want to fire at the animals unnecessarily. But there's plenty of opportunity to get close to them, and we do balloon trips too.' He opened the driver's door. The party climbed in.

'What are kids like that doing in a place like this?' said Amber quietly. 'They must have got the wrong holiday.'

Hex had been watching them too. 'They're rich kids whose parents send them to boarding school, then when they return home for the holidays they're packed off on some expensive trip to get them out of the way.' His voice was scathing.

'I think that's about hit the nail on the head,' said Gaston, and started the engine. 'I'm not very good at dealing with people like that, so Joe palmed them off on Patrick.'

'Any news from Joe?' said Paulo.

'He phoned to see what we're up to and to give us instructions about the visitors. Tessa's being pumped full of drugs so he's staying at the hospital for a while.'

Too late, Hex realized his remarks might have offended Amber: her parents had put her in boarding school and sent her away in the holidays too, although they couldn't exactly tell her it was because they were out on clandestine missions. 'Er, I–I didn't mean . . .' he stammered. 'Of course, Amber, your mum and dad weren't . . .'

'It's all right,' said Amber. 'I know you didn't mean to call my parents stuck-up rich bastards.' She gave him a smile like a cobra.

'I mean . . .' continued Hex.

'Just keep talking,' said Amber. 'I'm enjoying this.'

* * *

Gaston drove them to the water hole they had visited that morning. Paulo and Li noticed the others start to look around warily as they passed a distinctive baobab at the edge of an acacia wood.

Gaston noticed too. 'This is where the poachers ambushed you, isn't it?' he said.

Hex nodded and pointed to the sandy ground. 'Look – you can even see our prints where they got us out.'

'Was that really only this morning?' said Alex. 'So much seems to have happened.'

'You were lucky,' said Gaston. 'One of the wardens was killed last year. It was Patrick's brother. And Patrick and I got shot at a few weeks ago. If this continues, we won't be able to go on taking tourists around.'

Alex automatically scanned the scrubby bushes. He was looking for the tip of a weapon, the clump of a head camouflaged by branches, or birds startled by a predator. Once bitten, twice shy.

'Whereabouts did you see the elephants?' said Gaston.

'Just over there,' said Amber. 'Where those trees are.'

Gaston stopped the Jeep and put on the handbrake. He opened the door and got out. Alpha Force followed. 'OK, we're looking for elephant tracks. They look like this.' He squatted down and swept his hand across the sand in a circle nearly thirty centimetres across. 'It's basically a large, flat, padded print,' he said, 'and you might also see the toenails.' He drew several indentations at the front of the circle. 'Have a look around and see if you can find them.'

He stood up and folded his arms, watching as the group started to look around on the ground.

But Amber looked at him sceptically. She pointed straight at a row of broken trees that formed a passage into the wood. 'I'd say they went thataway.'

Paulo, Li, Alex and Hex groaned. They had nearly fallen for the trick.

Gaston grinned. 'Damn – that always works with the tourists. I usually get them looking for prints for ages. Yes, folks, elephants generally leave a trail of destruction wherever they go.'

He reached into the back of the Jeep and brought out the tranquillizer gun, a black tube and a couple of small cases. 'I'm going to load the gun now so we're ready.' He took the lid off the black tube and tipped out three darts. Then he laid the two cases next to the gun. Both contained bottles the size of alcohol miniatures. One set was red, the other blue. He took two red ones and fitted darts on the ends. Then he took a blue one and fitted a dart on that. He held up one of the red ampoules. 'This is the tranquillizer. It's strong enough to make a five-tonne elephant very sleepy. It's absolutely lethal to anything else, and of course that includes us.' He put the red capsule down and picked up the blue one. 'This is the antidote. If anyone gets so much as a scratch . . .'

Li finished the sentence for him. 'Give them the whole lot immediately.'

'Right.' Gaston handed Li the dart with the antidote and stowed the tranquillizer gun in a special rack like an umbrella stand on the outside of the door of the Jeep.

Another handy feature of ex-army vehicles, thought

Alex. It also had grenade pockets. It took him back: when he was small his dad had taken him to head-quarters and let him climb all over the SAS vehicles.

'One final thing,' said Gaston. He bent over, scooped up a handful of dust and stood up again, letting the sand trickle from his fingers. He watched it for a moment, then brushed the rest of the sand from his hands.

'Were you checking the direction of the wind?' said Alex.

Gaston got into the Jeep. 'That's right. We have to approach into the wind or they'll smell us and head for the hills.'

'All aboard for the trunk route,' said Hex as they climbed into the Jeep.

'Hex,' said Alex, 'do you get your jokes from some awful website?'

'Yes,' said Amber. 'It's called his brain.'

They drove through an acacia wood. Birds fluttered away from the vehicle. The ground was rutted and the Jeep lurched and bounced until they came out onto a plain. Ahead was a cluster of three elephants under an acacia tree.

Gaston braked gently. 'Hex,' he said, 'can you turn on the tracer?'

Hex flicked it on. The device vibrated gently, which indicated it was working, but the needle stayed where it was. 'These elephants don't seem to be tagged,' he said.

Gaston let the brake off and crept forward slowly. The elephants were standing quietly, their heads together as though they were having a conversation and had dozed off. One of them had her trunk neatly curled in her tusks. Alpha Force stayed quiet as Gaston halted again.

Still seated, he raised the gun to his shoulder and fired. There was a hiss from the gun and the dart hit the elephant in the side. The animal trumpeted in surprise, its ears fanning backwards and forwards. Gaston reloaded swiftly and fired again. His aim was good and he darted a second elephant just as the three massive beasts turned and stampeded.

The ground thundered; the leaves on the trees shook and the Jeep bounced on its axles. A massive cloud of dust ballooned up over the disappearing backs of the elephants.

Gaston holstered the gun back into position. 'I knew I'd never get all three, but two should be enough. They stick together in family groups anyway, so whenever we see these two the chances are that the other one won't be far away. We'll follow at a distance so we don't make them too stressed.'

'How long does the drug take to work?'

'About fifteen minutes.' Gaston started the engine.

When the dust settled, the elephants were visible as grey blobs in the distance. 'They've gone a long way,' exclaimed Alex. 'How fast can they move?'

'About twenty-five kilometres per hour.'

'Five tonnes, doing twenty-five kph? No wonder the earth moved,' said Hex.

Gaston eased the Jeep closer. Two of the elephants were looking less alert. Their heads drooped, their ears were less restless and their tails hung still.

The Jeep was now about ten metres away from the animals. The elephant who hadn't been drugged caught sight of them. Its ears fanned forwards and its trunk shot up in the air, probing. It turned on its heel and sped away.

The two drugged elephants barely seemed to notice. One of them fell forward onto its knees and stayed there, breathing heavily. The other folded its legs underneath itself and subsided to the earth. It lay on its side, its skin billowing loosely as it breathed.

Gaston took the Jeep to within three metres and cut the engine. 'We must be very careful when we go near them. They look sleepy but they might not be fully under. If we panic them they could wake up completely and run amok.'

Keeping an eye on the two doped animals, Gaston went again to the back of the Jeep. He loaded another dart with the red drug into the gun and passed it to Alex. 'That's in case the elephant wakes up when we get close. If that happens, shoot it wherever you can and all of you run away, fast.' He took out another case with a shoulder strap and passed it to Amber.

'We've also got to be careful that the undoped one doesn't come back. Families tend to protect each other. That's another reason why we've got the extra tranquillizer.'

The party walked up to the elephants. The one lying on its side stared up at them from a half-closed eye. The wrinkled lid blinked and the ear stirred, but aside from that the elephant didn't move. The other elephant, which was still on its knees, sank closer and closer to the ground until its head was resting on the tree trunk. Alpha Force were so close they could clearly hear the breathing of the two giants.

Alex had the gun at his hip, ready to fire.

'Are they asleep?' said Li. She was ready behind Alex, in case the antidote was needed.

Gaston nodded. 'They look fairly out of it. Right, Amber, give me that case you're carrying.'

She handed it over. Gaston flipped the catches open: inside was a small device like an ear-piercing gun. He picked up a tube and loaded the gun with two small discs the size of a small coin. Keeping the gun in one hand, he reached out and touched the elephant. The end of its trunk quivered. It registered he was there, but couldn't do anything else. He seized a chunk of its flesh in his left hand and applied the gun to it with his right. A brief click and he sent the tag into the leathery skin. It formed a bulge like a blister, with a clean sliced entry hole. Then Gaston turned the gun round and used a device on the other end to punch two staples into the entry wound before it had even had time to bleed.

'One down, one to go,' said Gaston. 'Amber, would you like to do the second one?'

Amber nodded eagerly.

He handed her the gun. She approached the elephant carefully and grasped a fold of skin at its neck. It felt warm and rough, gritty with sand. She put the gun into the fold and fired a microchip into the skin. It went in cleanly. She turned the gun round and sutured the skin as Gaston had done. The elephant continued breathing steadily, completely unaware. Amber stepped back and returned the gun to its case. Then she puffed her cheeks out. 'Wow, I just touched an elephant!' Her eyes were glittering.

Hex turned on the radio tracker. The needle

quivered and swung sharply over to the red area. 'It's working,' he said. 'They're transmitting.'

'That's our job done,' said Gaston. 'They'll wake up by themselves in a little while.'

They put the equipment away in the Jeep. Alex unloaded the tranquillizer gun and the unused ampoule was safely stowed in its case. Li dismantled the antidote dart and put the drug away too. They climbed into the Jeep and set off. Alpha Force looked back at the sleeping giants.

'Here comes the other elephant,' said Paulo. The elephant that had run away was appearing as a large shape on the horizon.

Gaston glanced in his mirror. 'Back to protect the others. She'll watch over them. We timed that just right.'

A sharp crack rang out across the plain. They had left the tagged elephants about ten minutes earlier and were making their way back through a tangle of acacia trees.

'That was a gunshot,' said Alex. 'Back that way.' He pointed behind them.

Gaston stamped on the brakes and brought the Jeep round in a handbrake turn.

'Is anyone shooting in the park?' said Li.

Gaston floored the accelerator. 'The poachers must have found the doped elephants. They won't be able to run away!'

12
AMBUSH

In the front seat, Hex was watching the radio detector as Gaston pushed the Jeep hard. 'We're close,' he shouted over the roar of the engine, as the needle inched towards the red. 'Closer . . .' But would they be in time?

Gaston swerved to avoid a clump of trees and they crashed into the wood, retracing the elephants' trail of destruction, and exited leaving a wake of swirling leaves and twigs. Alpha Force perched forwards in their seats. Where were the elephants?

A trumpeting sound blared out above the noise of the engine, furious and warning.

They saw the elephants ahead. The two doped ones were still lying down, easy victims for the poachers. Had they already been shot? It was impossible to tell at that distance. A coloured man in army fatigues was running, fast, desperately. Behind him the untagged elephant reared up and trumpeted, an ear-shattering sound of fury.

The poacher reached his vehicle, a battered green Land Rover, its roof covered with camouflage netting. The engine roared into life.

The poacher saw the Jeep arrive. He gunned the accelerator and swung the wheel round.

'He's trying to ram us,' said Gaston. He put the Jeep into a skidding turn and narrowly avoided the Land Rover.

'Yes,' said Alex in a low voice. 'He's trying to stop us following him and hoping the elephant will go after us instead.'

The poacher's vehicle surged towards the Jeep again and cannoned into its side. Gaston fought to regain control as the Jeep slalomed sideways, slipping on the sandy earth. He wrenched the wheel and the Jeep banged into the side of the Land Rover.

The elephant thundered towards them, its footfalls shaking the earth like the deep notes on an organ, audible in spite of the screaming engines. It gained on them in moments, more sure-footed than the vehicles with their spinning wheels and skidding tyres. The elephant's powerful chest was the width of two men, its forelegs like tree stumps. Its trunk snaked like a serpent over Li, Alex, Paulo and Amber in the back seat. The massive tusks loomed above them like scimitars.

Amber tore her eyes away from the spectacle behind them to look at the poacher, whose vehicle was so close she could almost touch it. He was bending down to reach for something on the floor.

'He's going for his gun,' screamed Amber.

Hex grabbed the flare pistol from the side pocket of the Jeep. The Land Rover surged ahead slightly. Hex raised the pistol and fired it into the poacher's windscreen.

Purple smoke blossomed into the cab. The poacher took his hands off the wheel as the smoke enveloped him. The Land Rover hit a tree stump and started to spin. The Jeep pulled away and the Land Rover clipped the elephant on the leg.

'Go, Gaston, go!' cried Alpha Force.

The elephant's full fury was now directed at the vehicle that had hit her. She got her tusks between the back wheels and lifted the Land Rover off the ground like a fork-lift truck.

Through the clouds of dust in their wake, they saw the vehicle tipped up at a crazy angle. The poacher tumbled out through the window, leaving a vapour trail of purple.

'*Dios mio*,' said Paulo. 'I had no idea they were so strong.'

'She weighs at least twice one of those,' said Hex. 'It's like nothing to her.'

With a toss of her head the elephant threw the Land Rover off her tusks like a toy. It crashed onto its side. The elephant swivelled her head. Her trunk snaked up into the air like a periscope.

'She's looking for him,' said Alex. His voice was full of awe. 'And she's thinking about what she's going to do next. Clever girl.'

'She's going to get him,' said Amber.

The poacher was on his feet and running, but the elephant was on him in a moment. One front foot crashed down on the top of his thigh and encountered no resistance. The poacher's agonized screams mingled with the sickening crack of his femur smashing. Then the matriarch elephant very deliberately stepped on the poacher's skull.

The cloud of dust in the Jeep's wake obscured what happened next.

Gaston drove until they reached a river. Then he pulled up and cut the engine.

Six faces looked around at each other, stunned. Gaston looked shaky with shock. Sweat was pouring down his face.

Hex was the first to speak. 'That poacher must have been watching us.'

'We'd have noticed him,' said Alex immediately.

'Yeah,' agreed Li. 'The wildlife would have given him away.'

'He must have had binoculars,' said Hex. 'He was watching us from a distance.'

'God, that's creepy,' said Amber.

Gaston had recovered enough to speak. 'That must be a new dirty trick they've learned. We'll have to be even more careful when we're darting them. We'll have to stay with them until they can get up and look after themselves.'

'Was that one of the poachers you saw earlier?' said Li.

'No,' said Amber. 'The black guy this morning was much slimmer and had a scar. I'd know him if I saw him again. I'd know all of them.'

'Gaston,' said Li, 'if that elephant had come back while we were still there, would she have gone for us?'

Gaston shrugged. 'You can't tell. It depends on whether they've had any scary experiences before. But it could just have been the shots that set her off. They've learned very quickly what shots mean.' He started the engine.

They followed the bank of the river. A herd of impala bounded out of the long grass, arcing through the undergrowth like tan-coloured dolphins.

'What if they've wounded one of the drugged elephants?' said Li at last.

'We can't go back and check,' said Gaston. 'It's too dangerous. By the look of things, the poacher didn't get that close before the matriarch started chasing him. It's actually quite hard to really hurt an elephant if you're not very close.' He drummed his fingers on the steering wheel. 'We'll tell the police he's there and they can sort out when to go and scrape him off the floor.'

Amber was gazing out along the river. It was cloudy yellow, like diluted paint. Obviously something had churned the water up recently. She straightened up. 'Oh look, we've got company.'

A boat was moored on the shore and she spotted Patrick with the three boys.

The one who had taken a liking to Amber caught sight of her. 'Hey, come and look what we've found,' he said.

On the riverbank was a crocodile snapped in two. The head, front legs and most of the body lay on the bank, its nose just touching the reeds. To all the wildlife that passed, it could have been alive and ready to strike. But the tail and back legs had been torn from it and left a few metres away. Strands of flesh, tendon and entrails poked out from the bottom of the body, as though it had literally been ripped apart.

'Did a lion do that?' asked Hex.

'No,' said Patrick. 'A hippo. They are much more dangerous.'

'They're the most dangerous animals in Africa,' said one of the boys.

'I thought buffalo were,' said another. 'Lone buffalo.'

It was Gaston who replied. 'No. The most dangerous animal in Africa is man.'

13
TROPHY HUNTERS

Li stood at the foot of the tree. The struts led up to the watch tower at the top. She took a breath. Her heart was pounding. Her palms were sweating. She hadn't even started climbing yet, and the very thought of the ordeal to come was making her freak out.

Get a grip, she said to herself. It's barely eight metres off the ground.

Telling herself not to be so stupid, she stepped forward, seized the rungs and climbed up to the top. 'OK, Li,' she said aloud. 'Now all we're going to do is come down again. No need to worry; just going for a little climb.'

But her nerve was wavering. It wasn't fear at being up there; it was fear of how she would feel once she started to climb down. It was the fear that she could no longer trust her body.

Li went into the hide and sat down on the wooden bench. She wouldn't rush it. She'd relax, look at the view, watch some animals for a while. She gazed out over the golden plain and the purple mountains beyond.

She had come out as soon as they arrived back at the lodge. Amber had been keen to do some exercise before supper, afraid that her injury was severely damaging her fitness. She suggested a swim and the others had accepted with enthusiasm. But Li couldn't face it. The others all seemed so carefree and confident, while she felt as if she was carrying around this terrible secret. The words she'd said to Paulo came back to her. What use was she to them if she no longer had her special skills?

She gave the excuse that she felt tired and was going for a lie down. Then she went to the map in reception and looked for a spotting hide within walking distance.

Giraffes made their stately way across the plain, their heads nodding. A herd of migrating wildebeest formed a dense clump of grey-brown against the golden bush. All of them had their own way of avoiding danger and solving life-threatening problems; she'd find a way too. But how?

For now, the ground seemed a long way away.

'Come on in, the water's lovely.' One of Patrick's group looked up at Amber as she came out in her dark-red bikini. It was the boy with the floppy dark hair. 'I'm Toby, by the way.'

Amber looked at him. He was just the kind of creep she didn't like. Too sure of himself, too sure she'd like him. His friends grinned at him, like lesser wolves in the pack congratulating their leader.

Hex came up behind her and poked her in the buttock. Amber whirled round, then her face split in an astonished gasp as she saw him. He was wearing the most ridiculous pair of shorts. They were orange and black, with jagged lines, as though someone had drawn all over them with several coloured pens held in a fist.

'Hex,' she drawled, 'what do you think you look like?'

'We're all the same when we're wet,' he said briskly. Before Amber had a chance to react he scooped her up in both arms. Then he let out a Hiawatha whoop, ran to the edge, pulling her after him, and leaped in.

They bobbed up to the surface at the same time, spluttering and gasping. Hex glimpsed Amber's face, lit with a clear desire for revenge, and powered off down the pool in a smooth crawl. Amber gave chase but Hex had already reached the end. He touched the wall, did a slick tumble turn and shot back past her.

Alex was sitting on the side. He'd got into the pool and swum ten fast lengths, but he couldn't shake the thoughts that kept whirling around his head after the encounter with the poachers.

Paulo came up to him. 'Penny for your thoughts.'

'That poacher was watching us and we didn't know he was there. We should have noticed. What's the point if we don't notice something like that?' Alex's blue eyes were steely. 'What do we do all this training for?'

'These guys are like terrorists,' said Paulo. 'I think the war's getting dirtier.'

The other boys in the pool watched Amber for a while, shouting encouragement and hoping she would notice and let them join in the game. But she was intent on racing Hex until he ran out of puff. In the water, her ankle didn't hurt much and she was enjoying every moment of the race. Hex accepted the challenge gleefully and showed no signs of flagging. The two of them powered up and down the pool like torpedoes.

Finally the three boys got out of the pool and walked over to Alex and Paulo. The blond one held out his hand. 'I'm Ralph, this is my cousin Toby' – he indicated the black-haired youth who had been trying to chat up Amber. 'And this is his brother Ben.'

Paulo thought Alex looked as though he wished they'd go away again, but he felt there was no harm in being friendly. He introduced himself.

'So, what are you doing here?' said Ben, sitting down on the sun lounger. 'You here for the game?'

'You could say that,' said Alex, a little curtly.

'We've been on loads of holidays together,' said Ben. 'Our dads shoot together and we've been shooting since we were small. Last summer we went to the Rockies. We were hunting deer and we took a pop at a bear.'

'That was me,' grinned Toby.

Paulo was shocked. 'You shot at a bear? Why? Was it going to hurt you?'

Toby shrugged. 'If it's there, you've gotta shoot it. Law of the jungle and all that.'

Alex looked at their eager faces as they boasted about their brush with danger in the wild. He was perfectly willing to shoot an animal if it was a question of his survival, but to kill it for fun was simply offensive.

Ralph didn't notice Alex's expression. 'I shot a stag in the Black Forest,' he said. 'It was huge.'

'That must have been difficult,' said Paulo, though like Alex he wasn't impressed. 'It's almost impossible to creep up on deer.'

'We had a telescopic sight, of course. Leupold Vari-X Three tactical scope. That's on my dad's gun. He's got a Blaser Lapua tactical rifle. Have you seen them? They're cool. They look really futuristic, all points and curves like my mum's Philippe Starck chairs.'

Alex's mind boggled at the whole idea of designer rifles. 'Er, no, I don't know them,' he said.

'Does your dad shoot, Alex?' asked Toby.

Alex caught Paulo's eye. A smile played across his lips. 'From time to time,' he replied.

'Oh, cool,' said Ralph. He obviously thought he had found even more evidence that Alex was a kindred spirit. 'What's his favourite gun?'

Alex savoured the moment. 'Nine-millimetre Heckler and Koch MP Five.' It was the submachine gun used by all the world's anti-terrorist units, famous for its reliability and precision engineering. Now he'd see whether these boys really knew their guns. Paulo was hiding his face in his hands, digging his nails into his cheeks to stop himself laughing out loud. Alex sat straight-faced, waiting to see if Ralph twigged what it meant if that was your favourite gun.

Ralph didn't. Instead he stood up. 'Hey, guys,' he said to Ben and Toby, 'let's show them something.' He looked at Alex and Paulo. 'Come with us.'

Alex stood up, bemused. Paulo followed.

Ralph led the group into the lodge, through the hall and out to the armoury. It was a large, window-less room lined with tall, locked glass cabinets. Paulo peered into the first cabinet. It held tranquillizer guns, standing upright on their stocks, each secured with fine chain and small padlock. The outside of each cabinet was secured with a more sturdy padlock.

Patrick came in carrying an AK-47, which he took to a long wooden bench in the centre of the room. 'Hi, Patrick,' said Paulo.

Patrick nodded in acknowledgement.

Alex watched, fascinated, as he began to strip it down and clean it. The AK-47 was a gun for serious battles, light years away from the luxury toys used by trophy hunters. Alex noticed that Ralph, Ben and Toby did not acknowledge Patrick at all.

Paulo was peering into a cabinet that held two hunting rifles. 'Look at the dust on those,' he said. 'They haven't been touched for a while.'

'That one's even got rust on it,' said Alex. 'Probably wasn't cleaned last time it was used.'

'They're relics inherited from the previous owners, when the place was a shooting lodge,' Patrick explained. 'We don't use the armoury very much for clients now; only when someone brings something they shouldn't have.' He looked pointedly at the three boys, but they weren't listening.

'Hey, Alex, Paulo, come and look at this,' said Ralph. He had opened one of the cabinets.

Patrick winked at Alex and Paulo and continued to clean his weapon.

Alex and Paulo went over to Ralph. He was holding a long, elegant hunting rifle with a telescopic sight. The woodwork had a dark-brown lustre like antique furniture. It looked expensive – very expensive.

'Isn't it lovely?' said Ralph. 'My dad bought it for me. It's a Dakota Seventy-six Classic, Safari Grade.'

'It's a professional hunter's gun,' said Ben. 'Lovely to use.'

Alex thought for a moment that Ralph was going

to offer it to him to hold, like a proud mother with a child, but the boy put it carefully back in its case, resting on its antique walnut stock, and wrapped the security chain around it. Then he closed the case and the outer padlock.

As they left the room Paulo and Alex said, 'Bye, Patrick,' but the others once again ignored him. Was that because he was black or because he was a member of staff? Alex wondered. These kids certainly could learn a thing or two about manners.

'So,' said Paulo as they headed through the lobby towards the pool terrace. 'You don't use that with tranquillizer darts.'

Toby spluttered. 'Good God, no. They confiscated our ammo but we've got more with us.' He lowered his voice. 'We're going to go out by ourselves tonight to drop a real animal.'

'It happens all the time in these places,' said Ben. 'Dad says you can shoot a lion and if they ever find it they blame it on the poachers.'

'Cool, huh?' said Ralph.

'We'd invite you to come with us,' said Toby in

a low, conspiratorial voice, 'but you need to have experience to do something like this.'

Two figures appeared silhouetted against the bright turquoise rectangle of the pool. Amber's willowy figure waved to them, limping slightly as she moved down the hall. 'Hey, there's Amber and Hex,' said Paulo. 'There's something I want to ask them.' He turned to Ralph, Ben and Toby. 'Would you excuse us?' Paulo's voice was icily polite, but Alex knew that tone. It usually masked the most ferocious loathing.

Alex and Paulo ran to meet their friends, eager to get as far away as possible from the boys.

'Been making friends?' asked Amber.

Alex caught her arm and steered her back outside. 'We need to do something,' he said in an urgent voice.

'Let's talk about it in my room,' she suggested.

Li walked in from the lobby area. 'You guys still swimming?' she said brightly.

'Something's come up,' said Alex. 'Did you have a nice sleep?'

Paulo thought that instead of looking rested, Li

actually looked more tired. She had dark rings around her eyes, which wasn't like her. Had she really been asleep?

But Li had latched onto the urgency in Alex's voice. There was a job to be done. She forgot her worries and professionalism took over.

Paulo also put his concerns to one side. But once this was over he would get her alone and find out what was wrong.

'They're planning to shoot a lion?' said Li. Her eyes were intense with outrage. Paulo and Alex had just described their conversation with Toby, Ben and Ralph.

'I knew they were scum,' said Amber. She spat the words out. 'Worse than scum.'

'How are we going to stop them?' said Hex. 'Shall we tell Patrick or Gaston?'

Alex smiled slowly. 'No, they have enough to worry about and I think we can sort this out. I have a plan. I think it will do very nicely.'

14
LAW OF THE JUNGLE

Hex and Amber were sitting on the ottoman sofa in the lobby, under a large tapestry of a leopard hunting. They had been there for fifteen minutes, watching the entrance to the weapons store.

Although the store was visible from the reception desk, no-one was on duty there and it didn't seem to be watched. It was evening and the phone rang only occasionally. It stopped after a couple of rings, as though it was being intercepted by an answerphone. Alex, Li and Paulo were in the lounge, keeping an eye on the three boys.

Footsteps approached. Hex grabbed Amber's hand and looked into her eyes. It looked for all the world like two youngsters on a romantic tryst.

'Your eyes,' said Hex quietly, 'are the shade of all the colours of . . .' He paused.

'The rainbow?' Amber finished his sentence. 'What are you on?'

'No, they're the shade of all the colours of plasticine mixed together. Sort of brown.'

'At least it's only my eyes,' said Amber softly. 'Your entire head of hair is that colour.'

Gaston walked past. He saw them and smiled to himself.

Alex and Paulo appeared in the lobby.

'OK,' said Alex. 'Li is flirting with them in the lounge. What's going on out here?'

Hex answered. 'All clear. No-one's watching the weapons store, and no-one's been by to check on it.'

'I reckon we've got about ten minutes before Li can't stand them any more,' Paulo said. 'Let's do it.'

He was wearing a belt-mounted toolkit, which he took off and unrolled. Inside was a selection of fine probes, like needles. He approached the door and kneeled down. Hex, Alex and Amber stood round in close formation to cover him and to keep watch. Paulo looked at the lock, selected one of the fine probes and slipped it in. Using careful, precise movements, he flipped the tumblers inside the lock and in moments the door was open.

Amber and Hex moved closer to the door and curled their arms around each other, giving Alex cover to slip into the room behind Paulo. Once the boys were in they pulled the door closed and moved into the centre of the lobby.

Inside the weapons store, Alex and Paulo lost no time. Paulo went straight to the cabinet where Ralph's gun was stored and got to work on the padlock. Alex opened a second toolkit on his belt and took out a slimline torch and an instrument like a fine nail file.

Paulo took care of the lock in moments. He looked at the gun in the case. He wouldn't have to bother with the second padlock and the thin chain. He could do what he had to without moving the gun. He opened the bullet chamber with the lever on the side of the gun, above the trigger.

Alex shone the torch in and handed Paulo the file. Paulo squinted into the narrow hole. He was looking for the firing pin. When the trigger was pulled, the firing pin rammed into the base of the bullet and detonated its explosive charge, sending it down the barrel at high velocity.

Paulo located the firing pin and smiled. He took the file from Alex. He had adapted it specially, making a rasping edge on the end, so he could slip it into the narrow hole like a plug. Paulo had also made a hole in the top of the file, so that he could thread another file in which would form a T-shaped bar to use as a handle. He slotted the second file into the hole, grasped the handle and twisted the file like a corkscrew, round and round.

Li was enjoying herself keeping the boys amused. The lounge had a pair of french windows that led out to the back of the building, into the floodlit yard where Moya's pen was. She persuaded Ralph, Toby and Ben to come out with her to look at the baby elephant. They didn't seem at all interested in Moya, but they were eager to keep Li's attention – and would have followed her anywhere she led.

She went and leaned over Moya's fence. The baby elephant came trotting over to her, ears forward. 'This is Moya, she's an orphan,' said Li. 'Isn't she adorable? But she might die because someone shot her mother.'

'That's sad,' said Ralph, although Li knew he really couldn't care less. 'But she's being looked after here, isn't she?' he went on. 'I mean, she'll be all right now.'

'No,' said Li. 'She needs her mother's milk. Look.'

Li put down her hand to stroke the baby elephant. Moya turned her head, drew Li's finger into her mouth and sucked, as she had done with Paulo earlier. 'Gaston just gave her her night feed but she's still ravenous. Look at her. She's skin and bone.'

Ralph was looking at the baby elephant. 'If she's that bad she'd have just died in the wild anyway. I know she's cute, but she's got to be strong to survive.'

'Yeah,' said Ben. 'The law of the jungle.'

'Anyway,' said Ralph, 'she can't know her mother's gone. My dad's dog didn't know its mother had died; we just got another dog and it soon got on with life.'

Moya, curious about her new visitors, tried to reach towards Ralph with her trunk. But she was still not quite in control and biffed him on the ear.

He yelped and stepped back, clutching the side of his head. 'That hurt!'

Good for you, girl, said Li to herself.

'Anyway, what's a nice girl like you doing in a place like this?' said Toby. He smiled, trying to ingratiate himself.

'Just seeing the sights,' said Li. 'Do you know, we saw an elephant kill a poacher today. The poacher was trying to shoot its friends. It went for him. Turned his Land Rover over and trampled him.' She watched Ralph, Ben and Toby carefully to see how they reacted. They looked uncertain. It would do no harm to embellish the tale. 'His head went *pop* like an egg.'

She had their undivided attention. She decided

to get a little closer to the bone. 'I've heard that lions can creep up on you without you even knowing. The first you realize is when they jump you. And then you haven't got a chance. Patrick said he saw a tourist with his insides on the outside. He was staying in a safari lodge in Kenya and had gone out to shoot a lion. Big cats always go for your entrails first.' She had made the story up from start to finish, but it was too good an opportunity to miss. Another gruesome detail sprang into her head. 'He screamed in agony for twelve hours before he died.'

Ben was the first to speak. 'Yeah, you've got to be prepared to kill or be killed,' he said. His voice took on a rough edge. 'That's part of being a hunter.'

Ralph and Toby agreed vociferously. 'Yeah, yeah.' They nodded in unison.

'It's the risk you take,' said Ralph.

'Hunt hard and hunt often,' added Toby. 'You don't get a trophy by quitting.'

'But why do people shoot these animals?' asked Li. 'It's pointless. You can't eat a lion.'

'It's the sport, the thrill of the chase.'

'Sport?' Li snorted. 'Anyone can kill something if they've got a gun and a great big telescopic rifle. It's hardly sport. You don't even have to get very close.'

'It still takes skill,' said Toby. 'Like being an assassin.'

'Except the animal can't shoot back.'

Outside the weapons room, Amber and Hex still lounged by the door. Amber kept an eye on the corridor and Hex watched for people coming through the main entrance.

Hex saw a figure heading towards the entrance from the drive. 'It's Patrick,' he hissed. Amber caught the urgency in his voice.

Music filtered through from the lounge. Amber leaned close to Hex and whispered in his ear, 'Dance. He won't hang around if he thinks we're having a private groovy moment.'

She started to dance, her hips swaying with the pulse of the beat. Hex caught her hand and twirled her around. She laughed in surprise.

'OK, Mr Smooth,' she said, her smile wide and dazzling. 'Try this.'

She did an extraordinary movement, which Hex could only describe as a body pop with a ripple. First her hips shifted, then her entire body shimmied as though her midsection had been replaced by rubber. Well, if she could do it with a bad ankle . . . He gave it a go.

Amber spasmed with laughter. 'You look like the funky gibbon. Let it go – get into it. Like this.' She did the incredible movement again.

Hex jigged one hip up and then the other. Amber shook her head.

Patrick had stopped and was watching them. Amber started to feel slightly on edge. Had he noticed something about the weapons store?

Hex had noticed too. They would have to talk to him. Making it look as though he'd only just seen Patrick, he said to Amber, 'I think someone wants a word with us.'

'Sorry to interrupt,' said Patrick and smiled awkwardly. His eyes were serious. 'Joe's back. I just thought you'd like to know.'

'How's Tessa?' said Amber and Hex simultaneously.

'She's had another operation to drain and disinfect the wound. They're worried she might lose her leg because of the infection.'

Amber gasped and her hand flew to her mouth. She felt sick.

Hex was equally shocked. 'If there's anything we can do . . .' he began.

Patrick nodded. For a moment he couldn't speak. He moved away, nodding. 'See you later,' he said. He was obviously very fond of Tessa, thought Amber.

He walked to the foot of the stairs, where he turned and stopped, his foot on the bottom step.

Amber's heart was in her mouth again. Amid the shock of Patrick's news, had they betrayed what was going on in the weapons store? Did it even matter now? Professionalism, she reminded herself quickly. Of course it mattered. They had a worthwhile job to do.

Patrick said, 'Joe wanted me to apologize for being such a terrible host and to thank you for all your help so far.'

Hex nodded numbly. 'It's a pleasure.'

Patrick walked heavily up the stairs. He never gave the weapons store a moment's thought.

Once he had gone, Amber and Hex stood still. Amber circled her bad foot, looking at it with concentration.

'How is it?' said Hex.

She put her arms around him and buried her face in his shoulder. 'I'm OK – but poor, poor Tessa,' she said simply.

In the weapons room, Alex's torch illuminated the wood on the gun's stock and fore end, the polished grain and the cross-hatching carved into it for grip. Without doubt it was a beautiful piece of equipment, like the dashboard of a Rolls-Royce.

Paulo, still filing away, glanced at Alex. 'Do you think that's enough?'

'A bit more, just to be on the safe side,' said Alex.

Paulo filed a little more, then withdrew the corkscrew and looked into the hole. He smiled. 'That firing pin is now well and truly useless. It looks no different, but if they pull the trigger, nothing will happen.' He blew into the hole to disperse the dust, then handed the tool to Alex.

While Paulo closed the cabinet and locked the padlock again, Alex checked to make sure they had not left any trace of their work. He wiped away some fingerprints on the cabinet. Then they went to the door and knocked once.

Outside, Amber and Hex had been listening for the knock. Amber went to the end of the corridor and checked: it was clear both ways and so were the stairs. Hex did the same at his end: no-one coming in from outside. He went back and gave two distinct raps on the door. A moment later it was pulled open and Alex and Paulo came out. Paulo pulled the door shut and kneeled down by the lock. Alex stood with Hex and Amber, as though he was chatting to them. The three of them provided Paulo with cover while he re-locked the door with his probes.

He straightened up. 'We'd better go and rescue Li from those creeps.'

* * *

Li saw Paulo and the others coming through the lounge towards the French windows. It wasn't a moment too soon. The guys were tiring of her lectures and she was preparing to change the subject to keep them there longer.

'Well, guys, we'd better be off,' said Toby. 'We'll leave you with Nelly the elephant here—'

'Moya,' interrupted Li. 'Her name's Moya.' It was probably an irritating thing to say, but she had to admit she enjoyed annoying them.

'Yeah – Moya.' Toby's voice was curt. 'We'll see you in the morning.' He led the way and the others followed him towards the muted lights of the lounge.

Paulo came out with Amber, Alex and Hex. 'How's it going?'

'I've just been doing my best to make them feel horribly guilty about shooting lovely furry creatures and big grey things with trunks. I think they'll probably avoid me now.'

'Well, they won't be able to shoot anything,' grinned Alex. 'That gun must have cost about four thousand pounds, but it's no more use now than a walking stick.'

'I wish I could see their faces when they test fire their weapons and realize their expensive toys are broken. That should put an end to their little expedition,' said Li.

Paulo was still concerned about her – she had looked terrible earlier. Should he try to get her on her own to ask about it? Not right now – it would be obvious to the others.

Amber suddenly remembered: 'Oh, we heard some news about Tessa.'

Li, Paulo and Alex caught the sadness in her voice.

'What is it?' asked Li quickly.

'Not brilliant,' said Amber. 'They might have to amputate her leg.'

Paulo and Alex were silent. Li said slowly, 'That's one of the worst things I can imagine.'

Moya wandered over to her water trough and dipped her trunk in. She made wet snuffling noises. She tried to suck, but blew instead, sending spray all over her head. She had another try. She put her entire head in, sending a wave of water crashing out over the side and onto her feet. She leaped backwards, hooting in surprise, then went forwards and did it again. This time she stood there as the water slopped over her.

'What on earth is that elephant trying to do?' said Alex. 'Drown herself?'

'She hasn't yet learned how to siphon water up into her trunk,' said Paulo.

Moya now had her mouth in the water and was lapping it up with her tongue. Her trunk was held straight up, like an aerial, the tips of it pinching together as she swallowed.

'Ah, bless,' said Amber. 'Do you think she looks any better?'

Paulo tried to look at Moya's shape critically. Was she looking any less bony, any less bloated around the stomach? 'It's impossible to say,' he decided.

'How many people and animals must suffer because of these poachers?' said Amber angrily. 'Look at Tessa, look at Moya. You know what, guys, if we could get these poachers we could make a real difference. I think we've found ourselves a mission. When Patrick and Gaston send us out tomorrow, let's look for ways to stop this carnage. What do you reckon?'

'Absolutely,' said Paulo.

'Agreed,' echoed Alex and Hex.

'A thousand times yes,' added Li.

'Right,' said Amber. 'We do it for Joe, for Tessa and for Moya.'

15
THUNDERBIRD

'Gaston's going up in a balloon to monitor the tagged elephants. Normally I'd go with him, but I've got other business to attend to. Would anyone like to go up instead of me?'

Joe Chandler had found Alpha Force in the lounge having breakfast. He looked as though he hadn't slept much. The sun streamed in through the lounge windows and highlighted the lines on his face, making him look older than they remembered.

It was Paulo who replied first. 'We'd absolutely love to go up,' he said.

'Yes please,' chorused Alex, Amber and Hex.

Li stayed quiet.

Joe seemed surprised by their enthusiasm. A smile spread across his tired features. 'Good. He can take three passengers.'

Li immediately said that she didn't mind staying.

'I'll stay too and feed Moya. You can help me, Li,' Paulo said quickly.

'Fab,' said Li.

Joe frowned. He pulled a chair out from another table and sat down. 'You know, you don't have to do all this. You can relax in the pool if you want – well, not this morning as it's got some nasty cleaning chemicals in it which you wouldn't want to swallow. But Patrick can do Moya.'

'Joe, we're happy to,' Paulo said. 'In fact when we leave, you might have trouble stopping me smuggling Moya out.'

Everyone laughed, including Joe.

Amber voiced the question that was on everyone's mind: 'This other business – is it something to do with Tessa?'

'No, it's a guest problem.'

Right on cue, Toby, Ralph and Ben walked through the lounge, each carrying a large suitcase. Ralph carried the ruined gun in a canvas case over his shoulder. They nodded curtly to Alpha Force and made their way to the french windows.

'Are they leaving?' said Paulo. 'They only just got here.'

'They are leaving,' said Joe emphatically. 'I am personally taking them to the airport. See that rifle they've got? They went out with it last night to shoot an animal. We'd confiscated their ammunition but they'd hidden some in their rooms.'

'How did you find out?' said Amber. She tried her best to make the enquiry sound casual.

'Gaston found them this morning. Their gun jammed and a lion chased them up a tree.'

Alpha Force looked at one another in amazement. Li let out a snort of laughter before she had time to control herself.

Alex shook his head. 'Serves them right. I bet they were in a state when Gaston found them.'

Even Joe was smiling. 'Yeah,' he said triumphantly. 'He thought they were poachers and he nearly shot them.' He got up. 'Listen, guys, I'll see you later. I'm dropping in on Tess on the way back – I'll give her your love.'

They watched his big frame as he crossed the room. 'I don't believe it,' Alex whispered to the others. 'They didn't even test-fire the weapon before they went out.'

Toby's voice floated through the windows. 'You can't do this to us; we're paying guests.'

They heard Joe's assured tones: 'Yeah, well, we don't need guests like you.'

'My dad will sue you,' said Ben.

Joe was not put off his stride in the slightest. 'Yep, I rang him this morning and he threatened to sue the pants off me. So I said I'd call the police. Shooting protected species carries a prison sentence in this country. And African jails are not nice. I can still call the police if you prefer.'

Alpha Force listened, trying not to laugh out loud.

As Joe escorted the boys to the Range Rover, he showed no sign of letting them off easily. His voice floated back through the lounge. 'And do you know why we don't shoot our lions and tigers any more?'

Alex laughed. 'How long is the ride to the airport?'

'A couple of hours,' said Hex. 'I reckon by the time they get there they'll think an African jail is preferable.'

'Li, Paulo, are you sure you don't mind not coming?' said Amber. She, Hex and Alex were wearing helmets, ready for the balloon journey. Hex was already in the basket and Alex was on the ground. He helped Amber into the balloon and then hopped over the side. The balloon towered up into the sky, a vast sleeve of orange segmented with silver, the burner roaring below it.

'No, I'm fine,' said Li.

'Well, I'll swap with you next time,' said Amber.

Gaston, also wearing a helmet, was checking the guy ropes that tethered the balloon to the ground. Already the basket was straining at its moorings, drifting to and fro between the three ropes.

Li and Paulo steadied the ropes while Gaston climbed into the basket. Gaston looked up and checked the burner. 'OK, ground crew,' he said to Paulo and Li, 'you can untie the ropes.'

Paulo undid the first one and released it, leaving two securing the basket at opposite corners. He and Li took one rope each, untied them and stood holding them.

'Ready?' said Li.

Gaston made a last check of the balloon. 'Let us go.'

'Three . . . two . . . one . . .' Paulo gave the countdown. He and Li released their ropes together. The balloon rose into the air.

'Hey, we're airborne,' whooped Amber. 'Up, up and away.'

Li and Paulo watched the balloon drift skywards.

'Come on,' said Li. 'Moya will be wanting her gallons of milk.'

Paulo thought Li looked tense as he followed her to the baby elephant's pen.

Before Li and Paulo had even set foot in the yard, they heard a trumpet of greeting. Moya stood at the fence, ears forward like tattered grey sails. As Li approached, the elephant reached towards her with the end of her trunk, the two fingers quivering. Li ducked, expecting a clout from a badly aimed appendage. 'Oh no you don't,' she laughed. Carefully, she put her hand on the end of the trunk. She didn't know if Moya would let her, but the elephant stood trustingly.

The skin was rough and wrinkled, like very old leather. Moya curled her trunk with pleasure and let Li stroke it gently. Li looked at her bony shoulders and puffy tummy and felt sad. This creature was so trusting, so sweet. Surely they could make her better?

Suddenly Moya gave a piercing hoot that left Li's ears ringing. She raced off towards the end of the pen, ears flapping in excitement. Paulo had brought out the crate of milk and was fitting a teat to the first bottle.

He laughed at the elephant as she charged over to him. 'Hey, good morning, little one.'

'Don't flatter yourself,' said Li, joining him by the crates. 'It's nothing but cupboard love.'

Paulo ducked out of the way as Moya curled her trunk towards the milk bottle. 'All right, all right,' he said, 'breakfast will be served in a minute.' Her reply was another ear-splitting hoot.

He aimed the bottle at her mouth. Her lips took hold firmly and she began drinking noisily.

Paulo noticed how Li's smile faded as the elephant settled into feeding. Under the surface, she was still far from happy.

'That balloon looked cool,' he said. 'Never mind; it'll be our turn tomorrow.' He watched her reaction.

Li was silent. For a moment Paulo thought she wasn't going to talk. When she spoke, she spat out the words. 'I am so pathetic.'

Paulo was shocked.

'I wanted to go up,' continued Li, 'but I didn't dare try. What if I'd had one of those funny turns in front of everyone else? Now it's not just a fear of heights. I'm afraid that I'll get afraid.'

Paulo let her talk. She was obviously finding it hard and if he said the wrong thing he might make her clam up again. Moya slurped the last of the bottle and he started her on the next one. She gurgled and flailed her trunk joyfully.

'Yesterday,' said Li, 'I went out to one of the hides. I decided I'd climb up and climb down again. Nothing heroic; just that. But of course when I got up there I couldn't get down. I was stuck up there for more than an hour.'

Paulo winced. '*Dios mio*, Li, you could have hurt yourself.'

'It was really stupid, I guess. But I can't even get up a tree. Soon you're all going to have to sack me from Alpha Force.'

'Li, listen,' said Paulo. 'The next time you decide to test yourself, take me with you. Then you don't have to worry about getting stuck. I'll help you through this. It's temporary, I'm sure.'

Li's voice had sunk to a whisper. 'I still have dreams about Dina. Every night. I'm up there waiting to go and she's lying with her back broken, screaming. She was as expert as me and she got it wrong. I might get it wrong too.'

With his free arm, Paulo pulled her close.

Something hit Li on the shoulder. She whirled round.

Penelope and Brains, the mother and son, were

using the tap, hosing water into their mouths. Thunderbird was looking straight at Li and Paulo. She shook her head, her ears flapping gently like the leaves of an enormous tropical plant, the sun punching through the two bullet holes. There was a hint of challenge in the elephant's eyes. She picked up a twig, curled her trunk around it and flipped it over to Li.

'She wants to play,' said Paulo, incredulous.

Li's eyes gleamed. 'All right, let's play.' She picked up the twig and tossed it back. The elephant picked it up and threw it again, her tail kinked out to one side.

Li exclaimed in delight. This wild animal was actually playing catch with her.

Then she was hit by two trunkfuls of water.

She shrieked and shook her head, her long black plait slapping from side to side like a wet paintbrush. 'Of all the sneaky things!' she spluttered. 'Thunderbird was distracting me so the others could ambush me!'

Paulo leaned on the fence and laughed.

At the tap, Penelope was refilling Brains's trunk.

Li picked up a bucket and vaulted over Moya's fence. It was more than a metre high but she managed it without a moment's thought. 'Right, this means war.'

She ran to Moya's trough, dipped the bucket in and chucked the contents at Penelope. The elephant shook her head and turned the tap off. Brains withdrew his trunk and levelled it at Paulo like the barrel of a gun and loosed the full load at him and Moya.

Moya reeled backwards, then decided she liked it. She closed her eyes and shook her head as the water streamed over her.

Paulo wiped his eyes. 'It's like a power shower. I hope they don't do that when they've got colds.'

'At least it's got all that milk off you,' said Li. She let Brains have another bucketful and looked for Thunderbird. But Thunderbird wasn't where she expected.

The elephant had moved away from the others, her ambushing role fulfilled, and was looking for other mischief. She had a definite purpose to her stride as she headed towards a double-thickness fence.

'Where's Thunderbird going?' said Li. 'What's over there?'

'*Dios!*' said Paulo. 'They've noticed the swimming pool.'

Li dropped the bucket and vaulted out of Moya's pen. 'Oh my God,' she said. 'The chemicals!'

16
TRAGEDY

There was a crash. Thunderbird stepped on the first fence and reduced it to matchwood. She bulldozed through the second without a pause.

Paulo dropped the milk bottle and gave chase.

Thunderbird walked up the grassy bank. Li ran after her. She was amazed at how long the animal's stride was. She looked like she was going for a gentle amble, but she really covered the ground quickly.

Li hurdled over the remains of the fence; then she had an idea. She stopped and picked up a piece of splintered wood from one of the destroyed fences and threw it at Thunderbird. Maybe she would stop for a rematch of their game.

The elephant didn't take any notice. She had spied a large body of water and was heading for that.

Paulo caught up with Li. 'She's determined,' panted Li. 'Do you think she'll come to any harm?'

'She can probably get in but she won't be able to get out. And I don't think the cleaning chemicals will do her any good if she drinks them. She might panic if she gets any in her eyes, particularly if she finds she can't get out.'

Ahead, Thunderbird towered above them, a black silhouette like the mouth of a huge tunnel. Her ears wafted serenely backwards and forwards, the bullet holes leaving an afterburn of bizarre streaks on their retinas.

'Anything you know about elephants would be really useful right now,' said Li.

'I know some jokes,' said Paulo. 'Uh-oh, here come the others.'

Brains and Penelope were making for the hole in the fence with a springy, eager stride.

'We can't block it off, they'll just knock it down,' said Paulo.

'Now all we need is for Moya to break out too.'

'Moya!' said Paulo. 'That's it! I'll be right back. See if you can stop Thunderbird before she goes for a swim.'

'Brilliant,' said Li as Paulo hared away to the yard. 'How exactly?'

She turned round. Thunderbird was on the pool terrace. She stood on a sun lounger and the metal buckled like wire. Brains and Penelope trotted up the slope, wanting only to join Thunderbird.

Li raced to the edge of the pool. Thunderbird was about two metres from the edge. She stopped, the end of her trunk pinching together as she analysed a smell. Was she getting an astringent waft of chlorinated water? Surely it must smell highly unnatural. But she didn't seem put off; she merely carried on sniffing. Li picked up a sun visor that had been left on one of the poolside chairs and threw it at Thunderbird, trying to distract her. The visor skittered round Thunderbird's feet. The elephant looked down and curled her trunk at it, still sniffing, but then went back to probing the water in front of her.

Brains appeared behind her. For a moment Li thought he was about to put his shoulder to Thunderbird's rump and pitch her into the water. But he didn't. Interesting, thought Li. So he and Penelope won't take the initiative – they follow Thunderbird. Typical of herd animals. The other two might not be a problem if they could get Thunderbird back.

Paulo came hurtling out of the poolside doors. He'd gone through the lobby so as not to run up behind the elephants and startle them. In his hands were two of Moya's bottles of milk. One was fitted with a teat.

Thunderbird put her trunk in the pool and splashed it around.

'Quick, Paulo,' cried Li. 'She's going to get in.'

Li knew she had to stop the elephant stepping forwards any further. She had an idea, but it was risky. It might encourage Thunderbird instead of putting her off. Or, even worse, it might provoke her to attack.

Li dived in and swam under the water like a torpedo, surfacing by Thunderbird's probing trunk. She had kept her eyes closed but the water ran down off her forehead and stung. She grasped the end of Thunderbird's trunk and pulled very, very hard.

Thunderbird careered backwards immediately, trumpeting and sending up a spray of water. She yanked Li out of the water. Li, amazed, let go and narrowly missed being gored by a tusk. As she fell back down she hoped she was over water. She hit the surface of the pool with a loud splash, and swam away in case the elephant decided to pursue her. When she got to the other end of the pool she turned and stood in the shallows. The elephant snorted, her ears flapped angrily. Brains and Penelope stood behind her, watching uncertainly.

Paulo offered Thunderbird the bottle with the teat. Thunderbird looked unsure. Then the smell of the milk reached her nostril. She reached for the bottle with her trunk in a gesture that clearly said, *Gimme.*

Paulo couldn't just let her have the bottle; he had to keep hold of it. He had to move in close. Would this fully grown, wild elephant let him, or would she feel threatened? She might easily be wary, particularly after what Li had just done. But Patrick had said that Thunderbird had been bottle fed. With luck, the smell of the milk would touch some memory and make her feel secure.

The tension in Thunderbird's posture seemed to melt away. Paulo held the bottle towards her mouth. She grabbed the teat in her lips and began to suck. Paulo said, 'Good girl,' and withdrew it. Thunderbird took a step towards him, looking for the delicious taste of childhood. Paulo held it just out of reach, and when she had taken another step away from the pool, allowed her some more. She slurped it greedily, just as Moya had.

He managed to get the elephant to turn round, and rewarded her again. She followed him down the slope towards the yard. After a moment, Brains and Penelope turned and followed too.

Li heaved herself out of the pool and looked around. The fences were flattened, the lawn was rutted with heavy footprints, one or two paving slabs in the terrace were cracked. There was going to be some explaining to do. But now that Thunderbird thought there was a trunk-pulling monster in the pool, at least they might not need the fences any more.

The balloon gained height rapidly, soaring over the plains. Amber, Alex and Hex leaned out of the basket, amazed at the panorama. Families of elephants lifted their trunks, sniffing the air as the balloon passed overhead. Buffalo poured from the woodlands into the shallow tributaries of the Luangwa. Herds of hippo stood in the water like shiny, overpadded horses, blowing plumes of spray out of their nostrils. Their jaws gaped at the balloon. A crocodile slithered off a sandbank into the water.

Amber had the radio detector. 'Hey, we're close to one of the tagged ellies,' she said. 'Quite a strong signal.'

Gaston kept a hand on the regulator while he scanned the ground. He glanced at the reading on the machine. 'Yes, that's a couple of ours.'

'That one's trying to push over an entire tree,' exclaimed Hex. 'Look.'

They looked down to see an elephant backing deliberately into an acacia. Two calves watched as the beast put all its weight on the tree. There was a groaning and splintering of wood and the tree crashed to the ground.

'They're destructive, aren't they?' said Alex.

'They do that when they can't reach the branches they want,' said Gaston.

'There is a certain mechanical advantage to weighing nearly five tonnes,' said Hex.

Gaston adjusted the regulator and they gained more height. As the burner roared, a herd of antelope scattered below. 'We've tagged about fifty elephants so far; today we want to see as many as possible to check they're all alive and well. This is the best way to see them as we can cover far more ground than in the Jeep. The detector counts the number that it's seen; we'd never manage it all by eye alone, it's too confusing. It will tell us when we've seen them all.'

'Hey, another bleep,' said Amber.

They peered over the side. They were over a water hole. Clearly it had once been much bigger; now it was a muddy indentation with a small patch of brown water in the middle. Four elephants glistening with wet mud raised their periscopes to the passing balloon. One of them ran up the slope, its saggy skin wobbling like an ill-fitting jogging suit. At the top it sat on its backside, stretched out its forelegs and slid down into the muddy pool.

'They look as though they're enjoying life,' said Amber.

'Li and Paulo would have loved this,' said Alex.

The balloon headed over a dry patch of savannah. Below, almost invisible in the golden grass, a pride of lions lay snoozing, a jumble of paws, heads, bodies and tails.

'Ellie ahoy,' said Amber, looking at the detector. 'I wonder what this one will be getting up to?'

Alex, peering out, saw it first. 'It's down here,' he said. The tone of his voice was grim.

Gaston immediately leaned over to have a look. He swore.

There was a mass of brown bodies tearing at a large heap of flesh: a clan of brown hyenas. The passengers in the balloon caught a glimpse of vivid red gashes in grey leathery skin. The prey was an elephant.

Amber felt sickened. 'I didn't think hyenas hunted elephants.'

'They don't,' said Gaston. His voice was grim. 'Something else brought it down; the hyenas are just scavengers. We need to get a closer look.' He pulled on a lever to open some flaps in the top of the balloon and let some gas out. The balloon sank. Then he took a flare pistol out of a crate in the bottom of the basket and loaded it.

'Cover your ears,' he said. 'This will be loud.' He pulled the trigger and there was a deafening bang. The hyenas scattered and stood at a distance, eyeing the shadow of the balloon as it slipped across the ground.

Alex, Amber and Hex looked at the elephant's corpse. At first they couldn't make sense of it. There were ragged holes all over the body where the hyenas had torn into the flesh. But there were also bigger wounds.

'Look at the head,' said Alex quietly. 'The hyenas can't have done that.' The head was a big mass of hacked meat, brutally disfigured. Bullet holes formed a small scatter pattern between the eye and the ear. Just below was a big, bloody hole where a tusk had been ripped out. There were large brutal slashes in the face on the other side too. The trunk had been hacked off and discarded. It lay next to the body like the carcass of a strange monster.

'Boudicca,' said Gaston softly to himself.

'We met her on the way in,' murmured Hex quietly.

'She'd been here for forty years,' said Amber.

'That's what the poachers do,' said Gaston. 'I'm sorry you had to see this.'

He closed the flaps but the balloon continued to descend. The hyenas slunk back and continued their meal. The air was filled with the sounds of their savage feeding – growling, grinding, whooping and cackling. Gaston opened the regulator and the roar of the burner drowned out all other noise.

17
A RICH STRANGER

Patrick staggered through the door, supporting a man on his shoulder.

Li, coming down the stairs after taking a shower, saw their silhouette. She sprinted towards them. 'Patrick, can I help?'

'Take his legs,' said Patrick, getting both his arms under the man's shoulders. 'We'll take him to the staff room.' Walking backwards, Patrick manoeuvred the man behind the reception desk and into the room beyond. 'We'll put him on the table,' he said, 'on a count of three. One . . . two

. . . three . . .' Together he and Li lifted the man onto the table in the middle of the room.

'What happened?' said Li.

The man was wearing a green shirt and dirty grey trousers. He shook his head from side to side, as though he was having a bad dream. One arm was hugely swollen; the whole of the forearm was bright red with purple blotches. Some of the skin was erupting in blisters. With his uninjured arm he clutched a dirty khaki bag.

Paulo rushed into the room. 'What's going on?'

Patrick explained. 'I was out on patrol. I found him on the edge of the road about a kilometre away. He was crawling along. I thought he was drunk, but he's been bitten by a snake.' He headed for the door. 'I'll phone the paramedics.'

Li leaned over the man. A sharp smell hit her as the man groaned and muttered to himself. 'I think he's probably drunk too,' she said. She tried to lift the man's bag but he grabbed it back. 'It's OK,' she said to him, 'we're just trying to find out who you are. Help is on its way.' The man gave a shout and clutched the bag even more tightly.

Li straightened up. 'Well, at least he's still breathing.'

'He's tried to put a tourniquet on,' said Paulo. 'Look.' He moved the bag aside to show Li. Just above the man's elbow was a dirty yellow bandanna. Paulo loosened it but left it around the man's arm. 'The course I went on said you shouldn't put a tourniquet on a snake bite,' he commented.

Patrick came back in. 'The paramedics are on their way.'

The man started to gasp. His face was clammy and pouring with sweat.

'He's having trouble breathing,' said Li.

'They said if this happened to give him an injection of adrenaline. We've got some in the emergency kit.' Patrick opened a drawer marked with a green cross and grabbed an object that looked like a pen. It was a syringe, pre-filled with adrenaline for emergencies such as snake bites or allergic reactions. Ripping the wrapper off, he looked at it nervously and prepared to plunge it into the man's shoulder.

'No!' cried Li. 'It's got to be subcutaneous for a snake bite. Here, let me.' Patrick looked only too pleased to hand the pen to her. She pinched up a fold of skin on the man's arm, above the tourniquet, positioned the needle at right angles to his arm and fired. 'If you do it into the muscle you might cause him more problems.' She passed the spent needle to Patrick.

The man suddenly went still, like a statue, his mouth open in a soundless O.

Li felt for a pulse on the man's neck. 'His heart's still beating.'

Without a moment's hesitation, Paulo peered into the open mouth. 'No obstructions,' he said. 'I'm going to have to give him the kiss of life.' He tilted the man's head back, held the nose and blew into the mouth. He gave three breaths, slowly, then tilted his head to look at the man's chest. 'He's still not breathing,' he said. He took a breath, leaned over the man and exhaled slowly into his mouth.

There was a commotion of people arriving in the lobby. Gaston came through, with Amber, Hex and Alex close behind.

Amber recognized the yellow bandanna instantly. 'My God!' she cried. 'He's one of the poachers.'

Paulo took another breath and blew into the man's mouth again. But his eyes looked confused.

'He's dying,' said Li.

'Serves him right,' said Gaston. 'They've just killed another elephant.'

'He's breathing now anyway,' said Li.

They hadn't noticed the other person who had arrived. Joe Chandler was watching from the doorway.

Silence settled on the room like a blanket. All eyes were on Joe. He must have heard everything. For a moment he did nothing – merely looked at the group around the poacher. Then he walked up to the table and pulled at the khaki bag the man was holding. The man tried to resist. Joe pulled it hard. 'Give it to me,' he said in a growl, and the man finally let go of the bag.

'Excuse me,' said Paulo quietly. 'I need to wash my mouth out.' He hurried from the room.

Joe unbuckled the bag – a design of diamond shapes showed through the accumulated dirt on the back. He tipped out the contents, threw the bag away and looked at the slim wad of notes that had landed on the man's chest. The poacher raised his eyes to him, wanting to take his money but not daring to move while Joe's steely gaze was on him.

Joe picked up the wad of notes and held it out between thumb and forefinger. 'Somebody else count this. It smells of blood.'

Alex took it numbly. The notes were crisp, still in the wrapper from the bank. He flipped through them. 'They're unused American hundred-dollar bills.'

Amber was watching him. 'There must be about a thousand bucks here.'

Li nodded. 'He didn't get currency like that from round here. Somebody must be financing the poachers from the outside.'

Joe leaned over the poacher. 'Where did you get this, scumbag?'

The poacher looked back at him with frightened eyes, but didn't say anything.

'Talk to me, dammit,' insisted Joe. He reached for the man's collar.

Patrick pulled Joe away. 'There's no way he'll talk to you, Chief. Probably doesn't even understand what you're saying.'

'We don't need him to talk,' said Hex. All eyes turned to him. 'The numbers on the notes are consecutive. That means they're traceable. I'll get onto John Middleton with the serial numbers and see what he can find out.'

Paulo had a bottle of Listerine, which he swigged at regularly and swallowed. He kept remembering what it was like being lip to lip with the poacher. The Listerine seared his mouth and throat, but it was better than that memory. He could still taste the cheap whisky and the smell of cigarettes on the man's breath.

The paramedics had taken the poacher away. Joe had called the police and told them which hospital he was going to. Now Paulo joined the rest of Alpha Force, along with Patrick, Gaston and Joe, in the lounge, to discuss what to do next.

'The poaching is out of control,' said Joe. 'As fast as we can tag the elephants, they're being killed.'

'Do you think it's all the same group of poachers?' said Alex.

'Were the elephants all killed the same way?' asked Hex.

Gaston shrugged. 'The way they were killed isn't significant. Yes, they were shot and hacked about in the same way, but it's just the best way to get tusks off a dead elephant. It doesn't mean it's the same bunch.'

'One lot set a trap – the one Tessa fell into,' said Amber. 'What about that?'

'Yes, that doesn't make sense,' said Joe. 'You don't catch elephants in a pit. The bastards must be after big cats as well. Still, at least we haven't found any more pits, so they must be concentrating on our elephants.'

Li was shaking her head. 'I thought this kind of thing died out years ago. Is there really still a big demand for ivory?'

'Of course there is,' said Patrick. 'And for animal skins. It pays better than farming.'

'Patrick, this isn't small-time poaching to feed a family,' said Joe emphatically. 'That scumbag had a thousand dollars. His family could eat for years and years on that. A thousand dollars is about twenty tusks. That's large-scale poaching – there's something big going on.'

'So,' said Alex, 'there must be a mastermind behind all this, paying the poachers. If we want to stop it, we have to find out who that is.'

Hex had his palmtop beside him. It gave a low vibrating noise. He'd got mail. He pressed a key to access his inbox.

'Is that my uncle?' said Amber, trying to read the screen over his shoulder.

'Looks like it,' said Hex. He scanned the e-mail. 'Ah, this is interesting. Those notes were printed four months ago and shipped to a bank in Hong Kong.'

'Hong Kong?' said Patrick.

'That figures,' said Joe. 'Most of the ivory ends up in the Far East.'

'This sounds like a very organized operation,' said Paulo. 'The question is, how did the money get here?'

'That poacher had been drinking, right?' said Amber. 'He'd been out celebrating. He must have been rather conspicuous flashing all that cash around. Perhaps someone saw him.'

Li picked up on her train of thought. 'We know

which road he was found on, right? Are there any settlements near there?'

'Not within the park, obviously,' said Joe. 'But I can show you a few nearby.'

'He came from Senga,' said Patrick. 'The design on his bag is something I've seen there. There's a woman who makes them.'

'We can't go asking questions around there,' said Gaston. 'I shot a poacher from Senga and they know me. They know Patrick and Joe too.'

'We could turn it over to the police,' said Alex.

'The police won't even bother to go there,' said Joe. 'No-one will tell them anything.'

'They don't know us,' said Amber. 'We can go.'

18
SENGA

Joe braked. 'If you get out here, Senga's about half an hour's walk. I can't take you any closer as the Teak Lodge Range Rover will be recognized.'

'Brilliant, Joe, thanks,' said Alex. All five members of Alpha Force climbed out of the Range Rover into the bright morning sunshine. Joe was on his way to town to visit Tessa and then give evidence to the police about the wounded poacher.

Alex handed lightweight rucksacks to everyone: he had packed food and drink for them all. Joe's eyes narrowed. Li realized he recognized them as standard kit from the adventure race. Tessa had had one too. 'Sorry,' she said. 'Bit tactless of us to dress like this.'

Joe looked at their walking boots and sun visors. 'No, it's good cover,' he said. 'The locals won't think there's anything odd about you – Tessa used to train around there all the time.' He put the Range Rover into gear. 'Look after yourselves, and I'll see you in a couple of hours.'

He pulled out onto the highway and disappeared in a cloud of dust.

Alex checked his compass against the map. 'Senga is this way.'

They started to trek through the tall grass. Soon they were surrounded by clouds of butterflies, sucking sweat off their faces, fanning them cool with blue and yellow wings. Amber felt her spirits lift. Her ankle was now more or less OK to walk on and she had missed these moments so much: just her and her four special friends in the wilds together. It was like winding back time to when they were training for the adventure race.

'How's your leg, Amber?' said Hex. He looked at her carefully, watching how she moved.

'A tiny twinge now and again,' she said. She was lying, a little; her ankle was stiff and sore, but it was something she could live with. 'I'm being careful, don't you worry.'

They walked up a wide track with trees on either side to the crest of a hill. On the other side, where the ground sloped away, was the village, a small cluster of round wooden buildings with thatched roofs.

'I think we should split up here,' said Alex.

'Good idea,' said Amber.

'I think we two should stick together,' said Li to Amber, 'and one of you guys come too. Then we won't look too intimidating a group.'

'I'll come,' said Hex.

'OK, Paulo,' said Alex. 'That leaves you and me.' He addressed all of them. 'We'll look around, see what we can find, and meet back here in an hour, right?'

The others nodded.

'You go first,' said Amber. 'We'll give you a head start and then follow.'

Alex and Paulo set off at a jog down the track.

'Bet they've been dying to do that for ages,' said Amber.

'You weren't holding us up,' Hex said.

'Come on,' said Li. 'I reckon we should head for one of those huts there.'

Paulo and Alex followed the track. 'Where do you reckon they keep their drinking dens?' said Paulo.

Alex recalled some of his father's tales of jobs abroad. 'Probably in the dirtiest, nastiest place imaginable.'

They were in what looked like the centre of the village. The track became a large flat circle of earth, like a small roundabout. Several huts were arranged around its perimeter. There was a big building like a farm shelter, with a roof of corrugated iron and one side open to the elements. A few rusted tables and chairs stood along the open side, some of them occupied. A man lay flat out across a row of chairs, snoring.

'Fancy a drink?' said Alex.

Paulo wrinkled his nose in distaste. 'No way Jose. Not even if you're buying.'

The building was raised off the ground. The floor was dusty, grimy wood. In the corners were heaps of dust and detritus – cigarette butts, dried animal droppings, twigs and dead leaves blown in from the surrounding woods. A counter ran along the back of the room. Alex and Paulo approached it. Paulo put his hands on it and immediately peeled them off again. The surface was sticky and left sooty streaks on his fingers.

Two elderly men were sitting at one of the tables. One wore a tall pair of green wellington boots with tweed trousers cut off at the knee. The other wore a bright red shirt with a big rip in the sleeve and a dirty stain of engine oil on the front. They looked at the newcomers with half-closed eyes, as though they had recently woken up.

Alex wondered if Paulo was thinking the same thing as him: were these two the drinking companions of the bitten poacher, recovering from hangovers?

Paulo walked towards them. Alex always envied Paulo his ability to turn on the charm, to make his face look so open and inviting that almost anyone would talk to him. When Paulo reached the table he squatted on his haunches so he wasn't looking down at the men. That would help put them at their ease, thought Alex.

Paulo started talking. 'Gentlemen, we found someone the other day who we think came from this village. He was injured so we took him to hospital. We're trying to find his family. Has anyone gone missing from here?'

The men looked at Paulo doubtfully.

Alex joined him and squatted down like Paulo. He added, 'Or did anyone drop in here, passing through? Maybe he came from somewhere else.'

One of the men turned to the other and spoke rapidly. They were willing to talk, all right; but neither Paulo nor Alex could understand a single word.

Li, Amber and Hex went round the back of one of the huts. A broomstick made of twigs leaned against a doorway. A tiny child, eyes deep-set in an ebony-coloured face, watched them as they walked past.

A woman came out of the wood towards them,

a plastic water carrier on her head. She moved sedately, like a giraffe.

'Look at that bag she's carrying,' said Li quietly. 'Same as the one our poacher had. Give or take a bit of grime.'

'Is it?' said Hex, mystified.

'Handbag identification and recognition – it's a girl thing,' hissed Amber. 'That's our lady.'

'Well, she might not be anything to do with the poacher,' said Hex. 'She doesn't look like she's rolling in riches. The bag's not exactly Gucci.'

The woman approached them.

Hex suddenly drew Li and Amber close. He whispered, 'What's that on her arm? Take a good look as she goes past.'

Li unfolded the map so that it looked like they were lost. The woman came alongside and Li nodded hello to her. While Li kept eye contact with the woman, Hex and Amber looked at her wrists.

The woman was wearing several burnished brass bangles – and what appeared to be an expensive Rolex watch.

When she was a few metres away, Amber whispered,

'I bet it's a fake. What would anyone here be doing with a real one?'

'More to the point,' said Li, 'where's the best place to get fake Rolex watches? Hong Kong.'

'Bingo,' said Hex.

Amber said, 'I know a bit of pidgin French. I'll go and talk to her – see if I can find out where she got it. Give me that map.'

'We'll be here watching,' said Hex.

Amber hurried ahead, half hopping to save her bad ankle. Hex didn't like letting her go by herself but she was the only one who spoke the language.

Amber rehearsed some phrases of pidgin French in her head. At last her enforced period of study leave in the back-up van would come in handy.

She caught up with the woman and called to her. 'Hello, can you help me?'

The woman stopped and turned. She was incredibly beautiful, Amber thought; the water in the carrier rippled in the sunlight and threw shimmers onto her shoulders like jewels from a crown.

Amber held the map out. 'Can you tell me where exactly we are?'

The woman took the map with a graceful hand, moving in the same unhurried way. She frowned as she looked at it, then glanced at Hex waiting with Li a little way behind. 'Doesn't your man know where you're going?'

'No,' grinned Amber. 'He's useless. Can't find his way anywhere without a computer to help him.'

The woman laughed. 'It's always the way.' She pointed at an area on the map. 'You're here.' As she brought her wrist up the watch flashed golden in the sunlight.

'That's lovely,' said Amber. She put her hand out. 'May I see?'

Proudly, the woman held out her wrist. Amber inspected the watch. It was a good copy but the second hand moved in little jerks; on the real thing it swept around the dial in a continuous movement. Amber had seen enough real Rolex watches to be certain that this one was a fake. 'It's really pretty,' she said.

'My boyfriend gave it to me last night,' said the woman.

'You're very lucky,' said Amber. 'Where did he get it?'

'He said it fell out of the sky.'

'Fell out of the sky? Where?'

Amber wasn't too sure if she had translated the woman's answer correctly; but she thought it was something like: 'Where all the money comes from.'

Was it a figure of speech or did the woman literally mean the money fell out of the sky – or rather, out of a plane? Amber enquired further, trying to keep her questions casual. 'Money falls out of the sky too? Where? I want to know so I can send my man there.' She indicated Hex with her thumb.

The woman shrugged. 'I don't know.' Amber sensed the conversation had gone as far as it naturally could without arousing suspicion. She doubted she would get more information if she pressed harder. She smiled and thanked the woman for the directions, and watched her walk gracefully away towards one of the huts.

Paulo and Alex were already at the rendezvous point when Amber, Hex and Li got there. They retraced their steps to the spot where Joe had dropped them off. Joe was there waiting in the Range Rover.

'Give me some news,' said Joe, opening the door. 'I've been battling with bureaucracy.'

'We think the buyers come in by plane,' said Amber.

Joe drove the car back out onto the road. 'That figures. All the parks have checkpoints and we'd know if any vehicles had entered or left. But where are they landing?'

'They'd need a landing strip somewhere,' said Paulo.

'It can't be on the open savannah,' said Li. 'It would be too easy to spot a plane.'

'They must have hidden it in a patch of trees,' said Hex. 'If we go up in the balloon and look at all the wooded areas we should be able to see it.'

'Hey,' said Paulo, 'does that mean I get a turn in the balloon? Cool.'

Amber dug Li in the ribs. 'It's your turn this time too,' she said. 'You'll love it.'

Li felt panic grip her throat. Her brain worked like lightning. 'I think if anyone goes up it should be you. Navigation is going to be crucial.'

'How did it go with the poacher, Joe?' asked Amber.

'The police want evidence before we can put that scumbag away because he didn't have any ivory on him.'

'What kind of evidence?' said Alex. 'Three of us were threatened by him.'

'I don't know what they want,' replied Joe wearily. 'I said he'd got all that money on him and it was directly traceable but they don't like being told their job like that. Besides, the system's riddled with corruption. I expect in a couple of days they'll be saying, *What money? He didn't come in with any money.*'

'Sounds as if we could do with catching something on camera,' mused Amber. 'People tend to take notice then.' The others nodded. But the same question was on all their lips: How were they going to do that?

'I take it the poacher is recovering well from his snake bite?' said Alex.

'Put it this way – he's in a better state than Tessa.' Joe's voice was bitter. 'He's even in the same goddamn wing of the hospital.'

'Can she have visitors yet?' said Li.

'Only family,' said Joe. 'She's still on intravenous antibiotics and they make her feel so rough that all she wants to do is sleep. I'll let you know, though, as soon as you can see her.'

Alex asked, 'Joe, how quickly do you reckon we can get the balloon ready?'

Joe reached for the hands-free phone on the dashboard. 'I'll get Gaston onto it so you can go straight up when we get back.'

Amber nodded. 'The sooner we find this airstrip, the better.'

19
RECONNAISSANCE

As they pulled up at Teak Lodge, Gaston and Patrick were on the front lawn inflating the balloon. 'Who's for the ride this time?' asked Gaston. He had to shout to be heard over the roar of the burner.

'That's us,' said Paulo and Amber together.

Gaston handed them helmets. 'Put these on.'

As usual, as many hands as possible were needed to get the balloon airborne. Hex, Alex, Li, Joe and Patrick held onto the ropes as the balloon gained buoyancy. Paulo and Amber stood with Gaston in the basket, watching him as he checked all the equipment.

'Cool,' said Paulo, looking around. 'I never expected it would have instruments. It's like a plane.'

Gaston gave him a quick run-through: 'Altimeter, compass, variometer – tells you whether the balloon's going up or down – and temperature gauge, which tells you how hot the air is at the top of the balloon. It's simple really.' He turned off the burner. The silence was instant and welcome.

Hex, holding onto one of the ropes, suddenly spoke out: 'I've got it!' His voice was excited. 'Joe, the poachers have built a receiver to find the signal your tagged elephants are sending out. That's why you're finding so many tagged ones killed.'

Joe looked sick. 'You have to be kidding.'

The occupants of the balloon had heard too. 'Joe, it's the only explanation,' said Amber. 'When we put a tag in an elephant, there was a poacher watching us through a telescopic sight, waiting for us to leave.'

'It's worse,' Hex went on. 'He could even have been watching us as we drove there. The tags would have been transmitting from the moment we put the batteries in.'

'Oh, that really is creepy,' said Li.

'How did they get hold of our frequency?' asked Joe, exasperated. 'You've seen their homes. Where do they get equipment like that?'

'From Hong Kong,' said Li. 'From their buyer.'

'Of course,' murmured Joe faintly.

'Get ready to let go,' said Gaston. 'Three . . . two . . . one . . .'

'See you later, guys,' said Amber.

'Don't forget about Moya,' said Paulo, looking at his watch. 'She'll be hungry again.'

As they lifted off, Li said to Alex, 'Come on – elephant duty.'

Hex turned to Joe. 'Joe, could I have a look at some of the tags?'

Joe showed Hex to a cupboard in the staff room. He lifted out a large cardboard box and put it on the table.

He began to unload boxes. 'These are the tags, and there's an unopened box with its labels in case they're any help.'

Hex picked up one of the boxes and read the label. Each carton contained fifty tags. 'You got a job lot of these, then?'

'We inherited them when we took over the lodge, like so much of the equipment.'

Hex took his palmtop out of its case and spread out his belt-mounted toolkit. He shook a couple of the disc-shaped tags out onto the table and selected a small probe from his toolkit. 'Let's have a look inside this baby,' he said and levered the cover off. He selected a small magnifying glass from his tool roll and peered into the workings. 'It's quite an old model.'

Joe pulled out a chair and sat down astride it, facing its back. 'Yes, they're probably smaller now. They're hellishly expensive. They have to be made of surgical steel so as not to cause irritation when they're implanted.'

'Interesting,' said Hex. 'It looks like this one's got a receiver so you can send to it as well as receive from it. What would that be for?'

Joe shrugged. 'Search me. I'm not very technical – as you must have noticed. The previous people had a lot of problems with the tags. They kept getting mixed up with the tags from other reserves. They'd think they were following an elephant and find it was a rhino or a lion. Finally they all clubbed together and hired a consultant to sort it out. He sold them new kit, but it had to integrate with the old tags because they couldn't go round replacing all the tags they'd already inserted. The mess was cleared up and they could all tell whose animal was whose, but don't ask me what he did. We're conservationists, not techies.'

Hex grinned. 'Well, if you kept getting mixed up between animals it was probably because your frequencies were too close together.' He looked up. 'Have you got any batteries?'

Joe lifted out another box. 'In here.'

'And is the detector in here too?'

Joe lifted out another box, still sealed. 'This is a spare one. Help yourself.'

Hex lined up a row of tags and batteries. 'Does your expertise extend to fitting batteries?' he asked.

Joe reached for a tag. In his immense hands it looked tiny. 'I think I can manage that.'

When they were all ready, Hex switched on the detector. The needle swung decisively into the red. One by one he took batteries out of the transmitting tags, to check that they were all transmitting on the same frequency. 'Just as I thought. You're transmitting on a set frequency. Was there any more equipment in that box?'

'Just a couple more hundred tags.'

'I reckon that consultant sold you far more of those than you needed,' replied Hex. 'You haven't got anything else – no other boxes; mysterious things that you can't figure out? We need the transmitter he used to programme them.'

Joe tipped the box so that Hex could see. 'Nothing.'

'Not to worry. I'll improvise.' Hex held up the detector in its bubble wrap. 'You say this is a spare? How spare?' His screwdriver was in the other hand.

'Well, it's been lying untouched in that box all this time. I'd call that very spare.'

'Perfect.' Hex tore off the wrapping and unscrewed the front panel. He lifted it away and looked inside. 'Oh, lovely old antiquey transistors,' he said. 'Now what shall we do with those?'

Alex ran into the room. His face was etched with concern. 'Sorry to interrupt – Patrick sent me. Joe, I think you'd better come and have a look at Moya.'

Joe got to his feet. 'Hex, I'll leave you to it.'

Hex watched them as they headed out of the room. That didn't sound like good news. But he had to put such thoughts out of his head. There was a job to do.

Alex led Joe out to the enclosure. Everyone was exactly as he had left them. Li and Patrick stood inside the pen. Between them was Moya, her head drooping, her eyes half closed. Her trunk hung down in a straight line, as though it was too heavy for her. It was the first time he'd seen the baby elephant standing still and it was a sorry sight. Her skin hung in shrivelled folds, like a dust sheet that had been laid over an angular piece of furniture. Nobody moved; they just stood in a sad tableau.

Joe stopped for a moment, taking it all in.

Alex stayed at the gate. Joe entered the enclosure and walked up to the baby elephant. Moya barely registered that a new person had invaded her territory. Her trunk didn't move, either in greeting or with curiosity; her eyes were still.

'She's gone the same way as the other one we had,' said Patrick quietly. 'The intestinal infection's too much.'

'Is there any point in putting her on a drip?' asked Joe. But his tone suggested he already knew the answer.

Li moved to the fence, stepped out of the pen and joined Alex. Her eyes flicked up to his: *Let's go*, they said. She sensed that Patrick and Joe needed to be alone to do what they had to.

Amber was in control of the balloon as it came in to land in front of the lodge. Her hand was on the cord attached to the vent at the top of the balloon envelope. When she pulled it, air escaped, making the balloon drop. They had been out for three hours and she was thoroughly enjoying it. It was like sailing, but curiously skewed – instead of manoeuvring the craft sideways, she could only move it up and down. If they needed to change direction she took the balloon up or down until she found a breeze going the right way.

Paulo and Gaston tossed out guy ropes to Hex, Alex, Li, Patrick and Joe, who were running alongside the craft. Amber felt the balloon lift a little in an updraught and let a little more air out. When they were out over the plains she had been able to let the balloon go with the wind. Now that she had people hanging on she had to be careful not to let it lift off again. Landing a balloon was just as much an art as a science, but Amber was used to reading the wind from her experience as a sailor.

The balloon descended smoothly. The moment it bumped the ground, Amber cried, 'Hold her down,' and opened the top vent fully. As the gas left the envelope, the craft settled down.

'Did you find anything?' said Alex.

'Nothing that remotely resembled an airstrip,' said Amber. She climbed over the edge of the basket and carefully lowered herself to the ground, trailing another guy rope over her shoulder. Paulo did the same on the other side.

'We've been all around,' said Paulo. 'There are no patches of jungle that have been cleared. It would have to be quite a big area and there's nothing.'

Gaston hopped out too. With everyone out of the basket, the balloon began to lift again. But that made it easier to move to its garage. The group walked alongside, each of them leading it with a guy rope, the balloon floating between them as though it was on a magic carpet. But by the time they reached the small shed Gaston had referred to as the garage, the envelope had lost a lot more air and was sagging over Paulo, Amber and Li, and the basket was considerably heavier.

'Just put it in there and we can unclip the envelope,' said Gaston. He went into the garage and came out with a roll of orange material in the same fabric as the balloon. He unrolled it on the ground like a sleeping bag, grinning at the assembled crowd.

'You're going to tell us all that material has to go into that little bag, aren't you?' said Amber. 'I knew there would be a downside to ballooning.'

Paulo was beside Li. 'You'd love the balloon, Li,' he said quietly. 'It's totally silent when the burner is off, like being a cloud. I can take you up if you like. It's not too hard to pilot if you've flown or sailed before.'

'Maybe, if we get time,' Li said, then changed the subject, her face serious. 'Joe's got an announcement to make.'

It was one of those moments when a quiet comment intended to be heard by just one person somehow caught everyone's attention. Alex, Hex, Gaston, Patrick, Amber, Paulo and Joe all looked at Li. Then everyone looked at Joe.

'It's Moya,' he said simply. 'Patrick and I had to put her down this afternoon.'

20
BORROWED TIME

Hex called everyone into the staff room. The radio tags were in a pile on the table. Joe, Gaston, Patrick and the other members of Alpha Force gathered around to watch him demonstrate.

Hex picked up one of the tags. 'The poachers have found the frequency of the tags we're using on the elephants, right? Now we can fight back.' He picked up the spare detector. 'I've modified this so we can change the frequency of all the tags in the elephants and then the poachers can't find them.'

'That's brilliant, Hex,' said Joe, 'but what's to stop them finding the new frequency?'

'I thought of that. Fortunately your predecessor bought some rather sophisticated tags, and we've got quite a few frequencies to choose from. If you change them regularly, you should keep one step ahead. Like changing your password on the computer,' he added. 'You do change your password on your computer regularly, don't you?'

'I haven't a clue,' said Joe. 'Gaston, do we?'

Gaston shrugged. 'What password?'

'How long will it take to change the tags?' said Patrick.

'We could probably do them all in half a day,' said Hex. 'We'll handle it if you like – you've probably got more than enough to do. We can set off at first light tomorrow.'

'Sounds good to me,' said Joe.

The next morning Alpha Force were up and having breakfast before dawn. They would take the Jeep – and the tranquillizer gun, which Gaston had insisted on giving them in case they ran into any trouble.

As they made their way outside, Alex asked Hex, 'Can we change some of the tags and not the others? It might be useful to have a few different ones around.'

'Absolutely,' said Hex. 'I rigged it up so you set the range you want to transmit to. To change all of them, you set it to maximum range – then every tag within twenty kilometres will change. But if you need to change just one, you set the range to just two metres or whatever.'

Alex smiled slowly.

'You've got an idea, haven't you?' said Amber. 'Spit it out.'

'Can you set one back to the original frequency the poachers were tracking?' said Alex. 'I think we should give them something interesting to find.'

'Stop here,' said Li. They were on the edge of a plain. In front of them was a grove of combretum bushes six metres high. 'This bush will make a perfect hide. Paulo, do you think you can get the Jeep in there for a bit of camouflage?'

'No problem,' said Paulo. He drove the Jeep into the thick foliage and cut the engine.

They were out on patrol to change the tags in the elephants. Paulo was at the wheel; Li had the modified detector. Alex carried the tranquillizer gun, loaded but with the safety catch on, and Amber had the antidote, ready to use at a moment's notice. But there was something else they had to do as well.

Hex had run a wire out of the Jeep's sound system. He connected it to his palmtop. 'Is everybody ready?' he said.

'Hit PLAY,' said Li.

Hex touched a key on his palmtop. The Jeep's speakers blared into life: the sound of lions roaring.

'Now we wait,' said Li softly. 'This is what my parents did on their lion study. They played sounds of lions feeding, mating and challenging each other. Other lions in the neighbourhood should come along pretty soon and see what's going on.'

'Is this the tape they used, then?' said Alex.

It was Hex who replied. 'It's not a tape, it's a download from a site.'

'Are you sure it's lions?' asked Amber. 'We might be playing leopards or cheetahs for all we know. Or some animal impressionist.'

'It's lions,' said Hex. 'I hacked into the computer at the Lion Study Center in Minnesota, where Li's parents worked.'

'In that case,' said Alex, 'they're probably saying in lion: "Don't come near, you'll get a dart in the bum."'

After about ten minutes Paulo pointed straight ahead and said softly, 'There's a lion.'

A large male with a huge mane stood less than sixty metres away. His chin was raised; he moved his head from side to side, searching for the intruder who had challenged his territory.

The recording roared again. The lion looked straight at the Jeep and trotted forwards.

'Ready with the flare pistol, Paulo,' said Amber, 'in case it jumps onto the Jeep.'

The lion slowed to a saunter, his amber eyes wide and his tail flicking. His shoulders hunched as he searched for the source of the noise.

Alex took aim, but the lion was coming head on. The only possible target was his forehead, but if he shot it there the dart might bounce off, or injure the lion's eye. Alex breathed steadily and waited for a better angle.

The lion trotted all the way up to the Jeep. The occupants froze. Li had assured them that the smell of the vehicle would cover their own odour, but would it work if the lion was this close? Paulo was ready to fire the flare pistol.

The lion sniffed loudly, taking in the strange smells of the Jeep. He was two metres long from head to haunch, his muscles rippling under the sandy coat. He moved round all the tyres in turn. Alex waited, ready to fire. Still the lion was too close. If Alex shot now he could wound one of his friends. He had to be patient.

The lion turned and walked away. Alex lifted the rifle and sent a dart into the animal's rump. The lion whirled and stared at the Jeep. Paulo's fingers inched closer to the trigger of the flare pistol. This was the most dangerous moment: if the lion associated them with the sting in his rump, he could attack.

The lion spat once, but turned and trotted away.

Paulo relaxed his grip. There was a sigh as five people let out their breaths. Paulo released the handbrake and inched the Jeep very slowly after the lion.

Five minutes later the lion sank to the ground. He sat on his haunches and put his chin on his paws.

'Paulo, take the Jeep closer,' said Li. 'If he's not startled by that, he's under.'

Paulo manoeuvred the vehicle up to the lion. The animal didn't move. As an extra precaution, Paulo revved the engine. 'He's out for the count,' he said, and turned the engine off.

Li, Alex, Amber and Hex jumped out. 'Keep that flare pistol handy in case his friends come looking for him,' Li told Paulo.

While Alex and Amber stood by with extra tranquillizer and the antidote, Li loaded a tag into the piercing gun. She grasped a fold of skin on the lion's shoulder and shot it in.

Hex checked the tag on the detector, then nodded. 'It's transmitting on the old frequency, so if the poachers go looking for our elephants they'll get a surprise.'

Alex clapped him on the back. 'Great stuff. Let's go before this chap's hangover kicks in. Where's the next elephant?'

'Quite close,' said Hex. 'A few kilometres that way.'

Paulo spun the wheel and put his foot down. It felt good to be driving again.

'You're enjoying this, aren't you?' said Li.

Paulo grinned. 'This isn't exactly a Ferrari, but it'll do.'

They had changed the frequency on quite a number of tags by the afternoon, and were beginning to make their way back to the lodge. Hex was still looking at the needle on the detector. 'There's another elephant over there.'

'There it is,' said Li. 'Uh-oh.'

Ahead was a fenced-off area, with a tangle of wire netting a metre and a half high nailed to stout posts. One of the posts had been trampled into the ground and the wire fence was bent down like a toy.

'Looks like it's another ellie who's gone where he shouldn't,' said Li.

'I hope that's not somebody's crops,' said Paulo.

'It's not,' said Alex. 'Look at the red tags. It's one of those areas where there are mines.'

The mood in the Jeep changed as though the temperature had plummeted.

The golden grass inside the enclosure had grown taller because no animals had been able to graze there. The elephant who was in there now was making the most of the feast. He wrapped his trunk around the base of some grass and pulled up a large clump, then swung it high over his head. Every time it thumped down on his back, dirt flew off the roots. He put the clean grass in his mouth and munched.

'We've got to get him out,' said Paulo.

'How?' said Amber. 'We can't go in there.'

'They're usually quite scared of people, aren't they?' said Alex. 'Every time we've been near them out on the reserve they've sniffed us out and run away.'

'But that's always been when there are poachers around,' said Li. 'Maybe it's something about them that they smell.'

'This elephant definitely knows we're here,' said Paulo. 'You can see by the way his trunk is twitching. But he's having too good a time to care.'

The elephant swished his ears and took a step forwards, reaching with his trunk. As one, the occupants of the Jeep tensed, expecting an explosion.

Nothing happened. The elephant carried on feeding peacefully.

Hex picked up the mobile and dialled. 'Hi, Joe? The new tags are working but there's an elephant in a minefield. What do you normally do in this situation?' He listened, then hung up.

'What did he say?' said Alex.

Hex looked shocked. 'He said there's nothing we can do. It's too dangerous to go in there.'

'We've got company,' said Amber.

They heard foliage cracking about twenty metres away. Three large heads appeared, ears swinging, trunks probing the air. One of the elephants had two holes in its ear.

'Thunderbird with Brains and Penelope,' said Li.

The three elephants walked towards them with a purposeful stride.

Paulo jumped out of the Jeep. 'They're heading for the minefield. We've got to stop them or they'll get blown up too.'

2 1
TRUST

'Try the flare pistol,' said Alex. 'That might make them turn away.'

The three elephants strode out confidently, unaware of the danger ahead.

'No good,' said Li. 'That might scare the one in there into stampeding. We've got to concentrate on Thunderbird – she's the boss. Paulo, do you think we can get her to turn back?'

'I'll try,' said Paulo. 'She came with me before.'

He approached the elephant. He was far from certain of her reaction. She might decide he was a threat. But she seemed happy to see him – her ears were forward and her eyes soft. Perhaps she remembered the milk he had given her.

She was now quite close. Would she let him touch her? He spoke to her softly in Spanish, soothing words he used when training the horses on his ranch in Argentina. '*Brava* . . .'

Thunderbird's trunk curled towards Paulo. She seemed to be inviting him to touch her. He reached out and put his hand on the base of her trunk. The corrugations in the wrinkled grey skin were rough ridges under his hand. The trunk fidgeted, probing him gently. 'I'm sorry,' he said, 'I haven't got any milk for you today.'

A loud trumpeting from the elephant in the minefield shattered the moment. Thunderbird marched confidently forwards, answering the call. Paulo ran after her. He got slightly ahead of her and looked her in the eye. She stopped, puzzled. Brains and Penelope, close behind, bumped into her rump and stopped.

Paulo put his hand out and stroked the ridged trunk again, speaking in Spanish. Thunderbird let him rub her face and stroke the ends of her ears.

Could he guide her away? She seemed to respond to him. But last time he'd had the milk to use as a lure. What could he do now?

Then a crazy idea began to form in his head. Could he climb up on her?

He grasped Thunderbird's ear. '*Brava . . . brava,*' he whispered. She didn't seem worried. With a mighty heave, he launched himself up her foreleg and shoulder, holding onto her ear and walking up her dusty wrinkled flesh as though it was a mountain. He swung his leg over and settled behind her head, his knees tucked behind her ears.

'I don't believe it,' said Amber softly.

'If he sees an animal, he has to put his backside on it,' said Alex.

The elephant in the minefield gave another hurry-up call, and Thunderbird set off. Paulo was caught unawares. He lurched from side to side; Thunderbird's neck seemed to pitch and roll in all directions at once. He was glad he hadn't eaten recently: it was like being on a ship in a very rough sea. He grabbed Thunderbird's left ear to keep his balance. She turned left.

He tried pulling the right ear. The elephant turned right.

'She's letting me steer her,' he called.

'Look, the others are following,' said Hex. Brains and Penelope fell in behind Thunderbird. Paulo decided to test how much they would follow her. He steered her first one way, then the other. Brains and Penelope followed.

'Just like horses,' said Amber. 'They follow the herd leader.'

'I might be able to use Thunderbird to persuade the other elephant out – what do you think?'

'You don't mean you're going to ride her in there?' called Alex.

'No, but if I take her close and turn her away, the other elephant might follow her out.'

'Why will he follow Thunderbird?' asked Alex. 'He's only interested in food.'

Li answered for Paulo. 'Elephants follow dominant females. She seems to be able to make the others do things.'

'What's to stop Paulo ending up in the minefield instead?' said Hex.

'Nothing.' Li called to Paulo, 'Be careful. If you lose control, save yourself first.'

'I think she trusts me to guide her,' said Paulo. He gave Thunderbird a reassuring stroke on top of her head, then steered her towards the hole in the fence.

The elephant in the minefield continued to eat, but was watching Thunderbird's every move. That was good, thought Paulo. If the elephant had ignored Thunderbird, there wouldn't be any chance he would follow. What he'd do was take Thunderbird up near the broken fence and then turn her away. He hoped that the grazing elephant would follow. And that there wouldn't be any mines in the way.

The elephant in the minefield gave a low trumpet and moved closer to the fence. Paulo's heart leaped: it was a good sign, but each time the elephant put a foot down, he might find a mine.

Hex, Amber, Li and Alex watched in agonized silence. The elephant walked towards Thunderbird. The ploy was working, but every step the elephant took towards safety seemed to take an eternity. And every move he made might be his last.

Paulo took deep breaths. He was as nervous as the others but he couldn't let it show. Thunderbird was a wild animal and would pick up his tension in an instant; if she sensed he was worried or stressed she might panic and stop trusting him.

Some sixth sense gave Li the sudden urge to encourage him. 'It's working, Paulo,' she said. 'Keep it up.'

Her comment came right when he needed it most. Inwardly he thanked her.

Amber picked up her cue. 'He got into the mine-field safely, Paulo, so he can get out safely. You're doing brilliantly.'

And it *was* working. The elephant in the mine-field was still walking towards Thunderbird.

Paulo got as close as he dared, then turned Thunderbird away. He talked to her all the time to encourage her, to tell her she was doing well. His heart swelled with pride at the trust she was putting in him.

'That elephant is coming, Paulo,' said Alex. 'It's working like a charm.'

Paulo looked round. The elephant stepped through

the hole he had made in the fence, twirling a clump of grass in his trunk, oblivious to the worried people all around him. Paulo took Thunderbird well away from the minefield.

'He's done it,' said Amber. 'Who'd have thought it?'

'We'd better help him down,' said Li.

But Paulo dismounted without any trouble. He rubbed the ridges at the top of Thunderbird's trunk, talking to her, letting her know how well she'd done. 'What a pity I haven't got anything I can give her,' he said. 'She deserves a treat.'

Alex, Li, Hex and Amber arrived beside him, watching Paulo praise Thunderbird. The elephant stood with her eyes half closed.

'She seems to be enjoying that at any rate,' said Alex. 'Do you treat all your women that way?'

'Look, here comes the other elephant,' said Amber.

The elephant was making his way towards them when something stirred in the bushes near the Jeep. The elephant whirled round in fright and went back the way he had come.

'No!' cried Hex. But it was too late. The elephant crashed back into the minefield.

There was a deafening explosion. Brains, Thunderbird and Penelope let out ear-splitting blasts of fright. Paulo dived out of the way as they stampeded. Clods of earth rained down from the explosion. The elephants disappeared in a blur of sand.

When the dust cleared, the five members of Alpha Force got to their feet.

'Is anybody hurt?' said Alex.

'Look at the elephant,' said Li.

He was still standing, but one leg was ruined. The mine had reduced it to a mass of meat. A large chunk of it was missing, as though a bite had been taken out of it. White bone gleamed through the glistening red. Blood from an artery formed a spreading lake on the sandy ground. The elephant tried to move. The top of his leg came clean away from the mass of disintegrated flesh. He crashed to the ground, blocking the gap in the fence.

'Call Joe again,' said Li in a stunned voice.

'The mine was right in the entrance,' said Amber softly. 'He must have stepped over it every time.'

Hex put the mobile to his ear. 'Hi, Joe. Bad news. The elephant stepped on a mine.' There was a pause, then Hex said, 'It's the leg. Totally smashed.' Another pause. 'Yes, we have. Yes, we'll do that.' He rang off. When he next spoke his voice was hoarse. 'He says to give it a tranquillizer dart and he'll be here as quickly as he can.'

The elephant lay on his side. His eye was still open and he was breathing very fast. His trunk twitched and flailed, his breath rasping shallowly.

They worked in silence: Alex still had the gun; Li prepared the dart and handed it to him; Amber stood by with the antidote. Alex fired at point-blank range into the elephant's hide.

The eyelid drooped, then closed. The desperate panting subsided, the sides stopped heaving and the trunk stopped jerking.

Joe was there within ten minutes, riding a quad bike. Strapped to the back of the seat was a rifle. He only had to glance at the fallen elephant to size up the situation.

'He's not going to make it. That wound will be infected inside half a day, even if he could walk.'

He unstrapped the rifle and took two bullets from his breast pocket. 'You may prefer not to see this; in any case you must stand well behind me. The bullets can ricochet inside the elephant's skull and come out anywhere.'

The five stood behind Joe. 'Will it be quick?' Li asked.

Joe nodded. He squinted into the sun and his eyes screwed up against the glare. 'Half a second. And you've made him comfortable with the tranquillizer so he's not suffering.'

Hex, Li, Amber, Alex and Paulo watched in silence. Joe walked up until he was less than a metre away from the elephant. The elephant was aware that he was there: his trunk pulsed slightly. Joe put the rifle to his shoulder, aimed and squeezed the trigger. Two shots went cleanly into the elephant's head, three inches behind the eye.

The trunk stopped questing immediately. It was a very quick death: two small red holes in the skull. They had all seen much worse during the actual injury.

Joe broke the breech of the rifle and walked back to them. 'We need to deactivate the tag.'

Hex already had the tag detector in his hands. 'Joe, we had an idea while you were on your way. What if we changed the frequency so that the poachers come and find him? We could wait here with a camcorder and catch them on camera. Then you'd have your evidence.'

Joe nodded vigorously. 'Excellent idea. Let's nail them.'

Alex looked at the surroundings. 'Why don't you guys take the Jeep – you can get the camcorder and grab us some lunch and I'll make a laying-up point in that clump of trees.'

'I'll make the hide,' said Paulo. 'I want to stay with him for a while.'

Li put her hand on his shoulder. 'Don't blame yourself, Paulo – you got him out. It was just bad luck that he spooked and went back in again.'

'Wait, wait, wait.' Joe put his hands up. 'I got over-excited. I can't leave you alone here if poachers are about. What if they find you?'

'They won't,' said Paulo. 'We can melt into the bush so no-one will see us.'

'No, come on, guys,' said Joe. 'This is one hell

of a nasty bunch of people we're talking about here. You saw what they were like yesterday.'

Alex replied for all of them. 'I remember it only too well – and all the other people we've dealt with over the years who are exactly like that.'

Amber added, 'We're very experienced at this sort of thing, Joe, believe me.'

'Look, Joe,' said Alex, 'why don't we try something? Hex hasn't changed the tag, so the poachers aren't coming yet. You guys could go back in the Jeep and get the camcorder while Paulo and I stay here and build a hide. If when you get back here you can see us, it's off. Is that fair?'

Joe's expression was unreadable. After a moment he said, 'This is *my* battle. I can't let you take these risks. You're no older than Tessa.'

Alex recognized the stubbornness in the man's face. He'd seen it on his father's face many a time and once or twice on John Middleton's. 'It's not risky if it's planned properly, and anyway, it's not just your battle. These animals are not just your animals, they're everyone's. We all want them saved, and we all want this park to be a safer place. This elephant's death has given us a way to do that. We simply can't waste it.'

Joe glared at him for a moment, then a smile played across his features. 'You must be the most stubborn bunch of guests I've ever had. What equipment do you want us to leave?'

22
THE TEST

Alex and Paulo watched the Jeep recede into the distance.

Joe had left them a spade and they started digging by the bush Alex had identified as a promising hide. Ten metres away lay the fallen elephant. Vultures were already settling on him.

Paulo stopped digging and listened. Just as he thought: there was a sound of cracking twigs and the rumble of elephants approaching.

A large shape passed the hide, then another, and another.

'They're back,' whispered Alex.

Thunderbird, Brains and Penelope walked up to their fallen friend. They stood around him and stroked him with their trunks, smelling his body.

Paulo and Alex stopped working and watched. Paulo had heard that elephants held wakes but neither he nor Alex had ever seen anything like it. Thunderbird put her tusks under the dead elephant's head and tried to lift him. Brains nudged him, as though trying to rouse him from sleep. Penelope found the ruined leg and ran her trunk all around it, never touching the blood. They made no sound; normally the elephants rumbled and snorted to one another as they went about their business, but now they were silent.

Thunderbird's exploring trunk found the bullet holes. She pulled away and stood at a distance. Brains and Penelope retreated too. It was as if they had realized something: he would never get up. Thunderbird led them away from the carcass.

Joe headed directly across country until he hit a road, then he followed it down through some woods.

The trees widened out. Li found herself looking at them. At first she had thought they were simply further apart, but she saw they had been cut down on either side of the road. Why would somebody do that? 'Joe,' she said, 'did you cut these trees?'

'No,' said Joe. 'I've never noticed this before.'

'I think we'd better have a look,' said Li. 'Joe, can you go really slowly?'

Joe braked and crawled along.

'The trees have definitely been cut down all along this stretch of road,' said Hex. 'What are you thinking, Li?'

'I'm wondering why someone would do that, particularly as it wasn't someone at the lodge.'

They travelled a little further and the trees closed in again. 'They're normal again now,' said Amber.

'I wonder . . .' mused Li. 'How much room you need to land a light plane?'

Joe braked in surprise. He looked back along the road. Then he reversed, fast. The engine whined.

'Look at the road, everyone,' said Li. 'If a plane's landed there will be marks.'

'Here they are,' called Hex.

Joe braked. Hex vaulted out and dropped to his haunches on the metalled road. There was a skid mark from a tyre, about thirty centimetres long. 'Just move back a bit more,' he said. Joe let the Jeep roll backwards. Another skid mark was revealed.

'My God,' said Amber. 'We've found the airstrip.'

Hex whipped out his palmtop. His fingers flew over the keys.

'What are you doing?' said Li.

'Just programming these co-ordinates into the global positioning system so we can find it again.'

'Right, Joe,' said Amber with satisfaction, 'where are Paulo and Alex?'

They were back with the camcorder. Joe looked around. There was the dead elephant, there was the minefield and the bush where Alex and Paulo said they would hide. But he couldn't see the boys at all. Even his quad bike was gone.

'I give up,' he said.

A thick bush trembled. Loose earth spilled out around the roots. Paulo and Alex stood up. They had dug a hole under it and buried themselves. Their faces were smeared with mud and Paulo had transformed his dark curls into a solid mass of mud and twigs.

'You can have the spade back,' said Alex and held it out.

Joe put his hands up. 'It's a fair cop. I didn't see you at all.'

'We've found the airstrip,' said Li. 'I think we should watch that too.'

Alex's face lit up. 'Fantastic.'

'Here's the camcorder,' said Hex. He held it out and then saw the dust and grime on Paulo's hands. 'Er – what's that?' Immediately he had visions of sand and grit and goodness knows what else getting into the sensitive electronics.

'You don't want to know,' said Alex.

'We brought something to eat and a few clothes,' said Joe, reaching into the Jeep. He distributed sandwiches and then handed over two camouflage jackets. 'They might be more comfortable than all that elephant dung.'

'Urgh – gross,' said Amber. 'Is that what it is?'

'It's dense, sticky and full of natural textures,' said Alex. 'What more could you want?'

'Alex,' said Paulo, 'you go. I can handle this on my own, and you might need to watch that airstrip. They'll probably come later, when it's dark, but we don't want to miss them.'

Alex nodded. 'You're right.' He looked down at his plastered arms and legs. 'Now I'll have to get all this off.'

Hex had reluctantly handed the camcorder to Paulo but his eyes were still fixed on it. 'I'm really worried about you handling that with all that crap on your hands.'

'It's not going to get inside, the camcorder is waterproof,' said Paulo.

'OK,' said Joe, 'we leave you here – you've got the quad bike . . .' His voice tailed off. 'Where did you bury the quad bike?'

'We couldn't bury that,' said Alex, wiping off his 'camouflage' on his T-shirt, 'so we put it all the way over there in those trees and stuck camouflage to it.'

'Good job,' said Amber. 'I can't see it at all.'

Hex clicked a button on the detector. 'OK, the tag's changed. The clock is ticking. Let's get out of here. Good luck, Paulo.'

Paulo had been waiting for no more than thirty minutes when he heard a vehicle pull up. He edged the camcorder back into position and began filming.

Two figures got out: one had black skin, the other was white. Ammunition belts glinted on their chests; AK-47 assault rifles were slung over their shoulders. They approached the fallen elephant, rifles ready, but one of them pointed out the bullet holes. They spoke one of the African languages, so Paulo couldn't make out any words, but he saw their surprise. The other pointed out the wounded leg and laughed.

They went to their vehicle and brought back machetes. The sun glinted off the blades. Paulo swallowed: he didn't want to see what happened next, but he had to keep filming. He moved slightly and rested his hands on a mound of earth to steady them.

The white man raised his machete and brought it down hard on the elephant's face, just beside the tusk. The sharp weapon went through the thick hide like a knife through butter. He cut deeper into the hole he had made and worked the blade down alongside the tusk. The other man grasped the tusk and started hacking on the other side.

Paulo felt sick. He kept the camera focused but tried to look at the faces of the men. The dark one had a distinctive scar on his cheek, as though a bullet had grazed his face at some time. The other wore a chain around his neck with a hyena tooth set in silver. Another scavenger, thought Paulo. How appropriate.

The tusk was soon out. The man with the hyena tooth yanked it hard and the man with the scar cut the roots. They dragged it free and dumped it on the ground. Time to start on the other one. Hyena-tooth went round to the other side of the elephant and chopped into the trunk. Three blows and it came away. Paulo wasn't sure how much more he could watch. Scarface threw the trunk to one side. It lay curled in the dirt. Paulo stared at it – that miraculous organ that was arm and hand, trumpet, periscope of smell, cudgel and shower head.

The second tusk came out more easily. The men dragged it and the other tusk to their dusty Land Rover and exchanged some words.

They looked at Paulo's hide, still talking, then walked purposefully towards it. Their machetes glinted in the sunlight, smeared with the elephant's blood.

Paulo's blood pressure hit the roof. They must have heard or seen him. How? He was well dug in and he had been completely still and quiet. His instinct was to run but he knew he couldn't. They would get him in no time; it would ruin the mission. He kept filming. He had to stay cool, believe he could remain invisible until he was actually rooted out.

The poachers were so close Paulo could smell their body odour, and the unmistakable tang of blood. He shut his eyes. In a moment a hand would grab his hair, or the first decisive blow of the machete would fall.

The poachers stopped just in front of him. Paulo opened his eyes. They were using their machetes to dig a hole in the ground. They went down about thirty centimetres, then Hyena-tooth reached down and pulled out a piece of tusk. Sand clung to it and a rag of flesh was still attached to one end. Scarface drew out another piece. It must be their secret cache. What a stroke of luck that he and Alex hadn't found and disturbed it. Paulo carried on filming.

The two poachers went on pulling pieces of tusk out of the ground until they had a big pile. When they'd removed all of them, they carried them over to their Land Rover. Then they got in and drove away.

Paulo got to his feet, easing the stiffness out of his limbs. He snapped the camcorder shut and headed for the quad bike. He had to return to the lodge with the camcorder, which was needed for the next stage.

Before he set off, he phoned Hex on the mobile. 'I'm on my way back. Get someone out to the landing strip now to keep watch. And start getting the balloon ready: I've just seen them unearth a cache of ivory and they must be about to make a sale. We can get evidence on the buyer too.'

23
UNDER COVER

Hex and Alex were ready as soon as they got Paulo's message. They bundled onto a quad bike. Alex was behind with Hex's palmtop. Locating the airstrip again was as simple as pressing a button. Alex was also properly prepared: he had put on camouflage face paint and disruption pattern clothing.

Hex headed across country at high speed. He skirted the tall grass so he wouldn't leave a trail that could be seen from the air, which might warn the poachers that someone had been near the landing strip. The fat tyres of the quad bike coped with the rough ground easily. Everything got out of their way: a herd of springboks at a water hole and a cluster of jackals feeding on a carcass.

Finally they burst through a clearing onto the road. Hex wheeled the bike around in a circle and halted. They were just at the start of the runway, where the lopped trees began.

'This is it.' Alex got off and Hex handed him a rucksack. 'Equipment check – have you got binoculars, mobile phone, energy bars, water?'

Alex checked the rucksack contents as Hex reeled them off, then nodded. He looked at the trees. Long grey pods hung from the branches, as though someone had decorated the tree for Christmas with grey frankfurters.

'I hope those aren't poisonous,' commented Alex.

'Li said they're sausage trees,' said Hex.

'Don't be daft.'

'She said they're not edible, so if you get peckish don't take a bite out of one of them.'

'They'll be good cover though,' said Alex. 'You know, it's a pity we haven't got a second camcorder. I could tape the whole lot myself.'

'No you couldn't,' said Hex firmly. 'You don't know which end of the airstrip they're going to land on. It's at least eight hundred metres long. You might be hiding here and they might do the handover all the way down at the other end. It would be a bit obvious if you came sprinting out of the bushes to film them. We can get a better view from the balloon.' He put his hand out. 'Oh, by the way, aren't you forgetting something?'

'Oops, sorry.' Alex handed Hex back the palmtop.

Hex climbed back on the quad bike and fired up the engine. 'Now get lost.'

Alex hefted his rucksack onto one shoulder. 'I'll call in every thirty minutes.'

Hex opened the throttle and the bike roared away.

Alex had to choose his laying-up point. There were plenty of places to choose from. He didn't need to have a perfect view of the runway, he just needed to spot a plane coming in and alert the others. That meant he could go quite deep into the wood, where he was sure to be concealed.

He walked thirty paces in and stopped at the foot of a tree. It looked sturdy enough. Alex jumped up, grabbed a branch that stood just above head height and swung himself up to a sitting position. He inched along until he could grasp another branch, and swung himself up onto that. Then he settled. They'd agreed that if he was there for more than three hours, Hex would come and take over. After another three, it would be Paulo's turn. But he really had no idea how long he'd have to wait. It would be dark soon too.

He could no longer hear the whine of Hex's quad bike. Now there was only the sound of the animals. With luck, the next thing he would hear would be the plane landing.

Hex took the same route back, sticking to the bare ground. He travelled in a halo of dust kicked up by the fat tyres. The river glittered in the corner of his eye.

His mind was full of the next things he would have to do. He had recharged batteries ready for the camcorder and a night-vision adapter to fit to it.

A small trench crossed his path – probably a game trail. Hex stood on the footrests, ready to jump it.

On the way there he had gunned the throttle and the bike had taken it with ease.

But this time the ground in front of it crumbled.

The front wheels crashed into the trench, leaving the back wheels spinning in thin air and throwing Hex hard onto the handlebars. Only the fact that he had been braced for a small bump saved him from going over them altogether. He collected his thoughts and revved the engine, but the front wheels spun and couldn't get a grip.

Hex turned the engine off. He'd have to turn the heavy bike so that all the wheels were in contact with the ground. Hopefully he'd only have to move it a little. Who would have thought a trench that was less than a metre deep would cause so much trouble?

He tried hefting the bike up by its handlebars but managed to move it only centimetres. He let out a sigh of exasperation. He definitely didn't need to be stuck at a time like this.

It took a moment for Hex to hear the animal approaching. At first, the silence after the roar of the bike was strange enough. Now he realized it wasn't silence.

It was something moving, something large that crushed foliage. Its digestive system let out low rumbles like an oncoming underground train. An elephant? Hopefully it would turn tail and run away.

He tried to shift the bike again. The back wheels inched down into the trench and the front wheels climbed. Just as soon as he had all four in contact, he'd be on his way.

A great bellowing ripped through the silence. That was no elephant.

Down the channel, something was racing towards him. It looked like a boulder, a rounded, greyish shape mottled with brown. Then it became a bulbous head with tiny ears, like the wing mirrors on a huge car. It had eyes like small polished marbles. A hippo.

Hex remembered Li's remark, way back in the adventure race: if you block a hippo's way to the water it will charge. And he remembered the crocodile snapped in half. He had to get the bike out – now.

With a roar that matched the hippo's for ferocity, Hex wrenched the heavy bike into the trench. It started to topple, sliding sideways down the bank. For a horrible moment he thought it would fall over, but it righted itself. Now all four wheels were on ground, but the machine was no longer facing out of the trench. It was facing along it.

The hippo was close enough for Hex to see the whiskers on its broad top lip. There was only one direction he could go. He gunned the engine and powered down the trench.

Enraged, the hippo gave chase. Hex's top speed was only fifty-six kph and the engine only 250 cc. Steering was an added complication – the bike bounced like a ball on the rough ground and it was a full-time job preventing it from turning over. The hippo was keeping up easily.

Ahead he caught a glimpse of sandy beach and a ribbon of dark water. The hippo showed no sign of tiring. It was fuelled by fury. Hex broke out in a cold sweat. What if there were more of them waiting in the river?

As he hit the water the bike lost speed dramatically and he nearly came off. He heard the heavy splash as the hippo followed.

Hex's wheels started to leave the river bed. The current was trying to take him downstream. He pulled the handlebars round hard, revving and revving. The engine spluttered. If it stopped, the current would drag him away. He paddled like mad with his legs – anything to help the bike along.

The hippo lunged towards him. Its mouth gaped open like a cavern. Hex glimpsed a sliver of tongue and vicious teeth.

The engine coughed, then roared. The wheels caught and Hex shot out of the water. The hippo receded in a cloud of spray.

Instantly his mind was back on the job. He had lost valuable minutes. Relief could wait until later. He checked his route on his palmtop GPS and accelerated towards the lodge.

As he roared up to the entrance he saw the balloon, a silver and orange globe taking shape on the front lawn. Joe, Li, Amber and Paulo were silhouetted against the balloon by the flare from the burner. The envelope was growing in front of their eyes.

The quad bike engine backfired and spluttered. Hex switched it off. The bike was covered with a crust of sand on the wet wheels and bodywork.

Paulo strolled over to Hex with an accusing expression, but before he could say anything Hex interjected, 'If you need a bike, don't use this one.' He grinned weakly.

'Hex, what on earth did you do to it?'

Hex passed him the palmtop. The GPS screen was still loaded. The map showed a red cross. 'X marks the spot. Don't go there – at least not until they've landed.'

A bleeping sound made them all jump to attention. 'It's Alex,' said Li.

Amber had the phone. 'Yes?' She listened, then said, 'OK,' and cut the connection.

'Well?' said Li.

'Just his first thirty-minute check. Nothing's happened yet.'

'The balloon's ready,' Joe told them.

Amber was studying the sky. 'We'd better get up there now so that we're ready to roll when the plane comes in,' she said. 'Look at the clouds. There's a breeze going towards the landing strip and it's our best chance.'

'Give me a moment and I'll get the equipment for the camcorder,' said Hex. He was running backwards as he spoke, then he turned and sprinted into the lodge.

Gaston passed him coming out of the main entrance. He was carrying two large packs, which he laid on the base of the steps. 'You're going to have a lot of equipment so you'll only have room for two people,' he said. 'Amber, you'd better pilot the balloon. You've got a real feel for reading the wind. You're a natural.'

'I'm happy to,' said Amber.

'I'll take the quad bike to get Alex after the plane's come down,' said Paulo. 'If it still works,' he added, with a glance at Hex.

Hex came out. 'One camcorder with recharged batteries, telephoto lens and night-vision adapter of my own design. It'll compensate automatically for lowering light levels. Don't worry about it – just film as normal.'

'I'll have my hands full,' said Amber. 'Someone else had better come to do the filming.'

Li took the camcorder from Hex. 'I'll do the filming.'

Paulo was stunned. He tried to search Li's face, but it was a mask. Had she managed to sort out her problems? Or was she forcing herself to be brave, like she had forced herself to go up to that tree house on her own?

'Good,' said Amber. 'It's better to have the two lightest people in the balloon.'

'Try to get pictures of the buyers as well as the poachers,' said Paulo. 'Then we can nail them all.'

Li nodded. 'Will do.'

The balloon was now fully inflated, straining at its tethers.

Gaston picked up the two packs. 'This is probably a silly question, but have you ever used a parachute? These are from when we used to have a plane here. I've checked them and they're fine. You'd better have them just in case.' He gave one to Amber and one to Li.

Paulo watched Li intently as she strapped hers on. She caught his eye and shook her head: *No, don't ask.* It didn't stop him worrying.

Amber shifted her shoulders to get comfortable with the bulky parachute on her back. She looked at Li adjusting the straps of hers. It was like a big rucksack. 'It's going to be a squash in the balloon with these on,' she muttered. 'I can see why we'll only get two of us in.'

'Put these on too,' said Joe. He handed helmets to Li and Amber.

The two girls climbed into the basket.

'Be careful,' said Joe. 'Those poachers are nasty.'

'We know,' said Amber. She smiled. 'This kind of thing is our job.'

Li agreed. 'Yes, this is our job. Let's go.'

24
SILENT SPIES

As Joe, Paulo, Hex and Gaston released the balloon, it rose quickly upwards. Within moments Amber and Li were three metres above the heads of their helpers.

Amber immediately checked the direction. 'That's the wrong way, so I'm going to go a little higher . . .' She opened the regulator on the burner, her eye on the instruments. 'If we aim for those clouds we can hitch a ride west. Li, how's the zoom on that camera? Is it going to be close enough?'

Li concentrated on the camcorder and nothing

else. She deliberately avoided looking at the ground and zoomed in on a tree about four hundred metres away. The tree jumped close and came into focus. 'Yes, it seems good. But the closer we can get, the better.'

'I'll do my best,' said Amber. 'I'm taking us up to a thermal that's going our way.' She cut the gas to the burner. The silence was sudden, total and surprising. Amber checked the compass. 'We're on course. Shouldn't be long before we've got the airstrip in sight.'

Li relaxed a little. So far she felt OK. This was a job she had to do and her mind was totally focused on that.

Amber was enjoying the silence and the view. The trees below them cast long shadows, making dramatic streaks on the landscape. The sun slipped down to the rim of the horizon. 'Wow, what a place to watch the sunset. This is amazing, isn't it?' She spotted some animals and pointed to them. 'Look, there are some zebras hiding in the middle of that herd of wildebeest. They must be trying not to be seen. Not exactly inconspicuous, are they?'

Li looked out. Panic sounded in her head like a tom-tom drum, but after a moment it subsided. She began to take in what she was seeing. In the midst of the chocolate-brown wildebeest were two vibrant striped coats. 'That's surreal,' she said. 'As though someone has set it up for an advert about standing out in the crowd.'

'Take some film of it,' said Amber. 'It would make the cover of *National Geographic*.'

Li started on a close-up of the zebra and panned out to the wildebeest around it. 'We could be award-winning wildlife photographers by day and secret agents by night,' she giggled. 'Better not use up all the batteries, though,' she added, and switched the camcorder off.

'Hey, look,' said Amber. Her voice was a whisper.

A black shape appeared out of the clouds, like an object surfacing from a lake. It became wheels, then an undercarriage, then the white belly of a light plane. The sound of its engines washed over them like a wave.

'Is that them?' whispered Amber.

Li put the camcorder to her eye and pointed it at

the ground. 'I'll pretend to be filming animals,' she said, 'in case they can see us.'

Amber kept an eye on the plane. It was losing height rapidly. 'Looks like it might be about to land,' she said.

The balloon started drifting backwards, away from the plane. 'Darn,' said Amber. She opened the regulator. 'We've got caught in an air current. It's pushing us away. I'll have to get higher and hop on a current going back that way.'

'Is it the backdraught from the plane?' asked Li, still pretending to film wildebeest.

'I don't think so,' said Amber. 'A plane like that is too small to have much of an effect. It might be caused by the road, though; or the cleared area where the runway is.'

The plane slipped down between the trees, heading for the landing strip. But the balloon seemed to be drifting further away, like a twig in a stream whirling helplessly in the wake of a passing boat.

The mobile phone quivered in Li's pocket. She had set it to vibrate rather than ring, in case a call attracted attention. She put the phone to her ear. 'Yes?'

It was Hex. 'Alex just called. The plane's coming in. It's going to land at the north end.'

'We know,' said Li. 'We're trying to get over there but steering isn't that simple.'

'Hey, we've got ballast,' said Amber. She was holding a sandbag. 'Let's throw these out – we'll rise faster.'

Alex heard the plane before he saw it. For a while all he had been aware of was the dusk chorus of the animals and the ultrasonic squeaks of bats as they flocked to the long pods hanging from the sausage trees. Then the whine of the engine came as clear as day, getting lower and lower, like a descending scale on a piano. The plane was definitely coming down into the gap between the trees. He made his call to Hex then; the girls needed as much time as possible to get into position.

The plane landed at the other end of the strip. By the time the white fuselage glided past Alex, it was almost at a standstill. The tips of the wings nearly grazed the trees. That pilot must be very good, he thought, to bring the plane in so precisely each time in such a tight space.

Of more concern to Alex, though, the plane had stopped right opposite where he was hiding.

Alex's mind raced. Should he try to get further away? No, that would definitely alert them. He was wearing camouflage, he was high up in a tree with a good covering of leaves and those dangling sausage things. He just had to stay still. He cursed that he hadn't got a camcorder. He would have had an excellent view.

The plane had two occupants. One was the pilot. That figured: even if the buyer could fly, it was unlikely that he would have the kind of precision skills needed to land in a place like this.

The cockpit door opened and a figure stepped out. In the dusk it was hard to see him clearly but his build was slight. He looked up and down the airfield and checked the time. His diamond-encrusted watch caught the last rays of sunlight.

A vehicle was approaching. A Land Rover. Alex heard the handbrake rasp and the engine die. Two figures got out.

Their faces were in shadow but Alex recognized them by the way they moved. They were two of the poachers who had threatened them that first morning. He could see the stubby silhouettes of AK-47s swinging from their shoulders.

The poachers hefted a couple of sacks from the back seat of the Land Rover and walked towards the man who had climbed out of the plane.

Alex wasn't close enough to hear what they were saying, but they weren't speaking English. He caught the odd word, more a flavour of the language than the language itself. It sounded like French. Didn't Amber say that quite a lot of people in Zambia spoke pidgin French?

The poachers handed over one of the sacks. The transaction was starting. Alex glanced up through the trees to the sky. He couldn't see whether the balloon was there or not. He hoped it was.

Amber watched the compass. They were drifting east and they needed to go north. The burner was on, taking them higher. Then suddenly their direction changed. 'That's it,' she exclaimed, and stopped the burner. She peered down. 'We should be over the runway in about thirty seconds.'

'I'm ready,' said Li. She was poised over the basket, the camcorder on pause and ready to film as soon as the poachers came into view.

Amber was studying the trees. 'It's quite still down there. I reckon as soon as we're over the road we could go lower.'

The runway appeared below them. The layout was so obvious from the air once they knew what it was; the trees widened like an avenue, split by the dusty ribbon of road. There was the plane, like a white cross in the middle. Tiny figures stood beside it, just visible in the gloom.

Amber pulled the vent and let air out of the top of the balloon. They were going in.

Li lost no time. She zoomed to maximum. The image appeared in monochrome as Hex's night-vision adapter kicked in. 'Two poachers,' she said quietly, 'with guns. One buyer – possibly oriental, as we suspected. Amber, how low can you go? I can't get their faces from here.'

Amber pulled on the vent again. The balloon

plummeted. Li felt panic squeezing her heart. She was falling. She saw Dina and the rock face, the horrible silent vision from her dreams. The camera started to shake in her hands.

Amber closed the vent hurriedly. 'Sorry. Wind's a bit unpredictable between these trees.'

Li took deep breaths. Sweat ran in cold rivulets down her back. Concentrate on filming, she told herself. Do the job. The balloon will be OK. Amber knows what she's doing.

She steadied the camera on the rim of the basket and focused. She would be so very relieved when they were back on solid ground.

She filmed the buyer taking a sack from one of the poachers. He tipped it out onto the ground. The contents looked like a pile of pale blocks. They became ivory, hollow like sections of a pipe, some pointed at the end, some still bearing dark shreds of flesh. The balloon was still drifting down.

'Tell me when you've got enough,' whispered Amber. 'I daren't use the burner until we're finished because they might hear.'

'I've got their faces now,' said Li. She filmed the

man with the scar like a crater in the middle of his cheek. His skin looked grey in the monochrome night-vision filter. Then she got the paler man wearing the hyena tooth around his neck.

Amber looked at the altimeter. They were at thirty metres. Even without the benefit of the zoom lens and the night-vision adapter, Amber had seen the black outlines of guns on the poachers' shoulders. The balloon was easily within firing range. She had her hand on the burner control, ready to lift the balloon out as soon as Li gave the word.

Li seemed to read her thoughts. 'I just want them to hand over the money,' she said. 'Otherwise we don't get the buyer.'

Now that Li was intent on filming, her worries had disappeared. The buyer was squatting on the ground, packing the hacked-up tusks into the sack. Li filmed his expensive watch, flashing diamonds even in the dim evening light. She caught his crisp suit – probably linen, and most likely hand tailored. She made sure she filmed the pilot, dressed in a pale safari jacket and watching every moment of the transaction. Was he a bodyguard? He had a short, stubby pistol in a holster on his hip – no doubt to discourage the poachers in case they tried to keep the ivory as well as the money. She also got a clear shot of the plane's registration number. All good evidence.

The buyer reached into his inside pocket. Li wanted to whoop with triumph. This was the moment. He took out a fat envelope and handed it to Hyena-tooth. The poacher ripped the envelope open and pulled out a wad of notes. Li filmed them as he flipped through the stack; they were hundred-dollar bills. The poacher nodded and folded the notes into the pocket of his combat trousers. Li had got it all.

She switched off the power and put the lens cap on.

Then Amber gave her the bad news: 'We're going to have to drift out. We're too low to use the burner. They'll hear and they'll see us.'

Li nodded.

Amber watched the instruments, her face a mask of concentration. She felt a gentle breeze on her face, but instead of taking them up, it carried them along the path of the runway.

Below them, the buyer and the pilot were getting into the plane. The balloon drifted down even further.

Li whispered to Amber, her voice urgent. 'They'll see us when they take off. We'll have to use the burner, while we've still got the element of surprise.'

Amber tried to think of another solution but Li was right. The balloon wasn't going to get them out of trouble; it was taking them towards it.

She fired the burner. It flared bright blue. The sound seemed recklessly loud.

All four men on the ground looked up, shocked. The pilot whipped out his pistol. Both poachers swung their AK-47s into action and fired.

Amber and Li ducked down inside the basket. Li looked up at the burner, flaring bright blue against the navy sky. 'Is it going as fast as it can?' she gasped.

'Yes,' shouted Amber.

A bullet ripped through the basket, leaving a smouldering hole in the wicker. Amber screamed. Li folded her body around the camcorder; she had to protect it at all costs.

'You hit?' gasped Li.

'No,' said Amber.

Li looked up at the burner and its supports silhouetted against the sky. It all seemed so fragile. Slender struts and suspension cables were all that held the balloon together. 'What if we're hit?' she said. 'What if they put a hole in us?'

Amber kneeled up and managed a peek at the altimeter. A bullet dinged off it and she threw herself back onto the floor. 'We're going up fast.' She swallowed and tried to sound calm. 'We should be out of range soon.' Then she winced.

'What is it?' asked Li. 'Are you hit?'

'No,' said Amber. 'But I just realized those cylinders hanging around the outside of the basket are spare tanks of propane for the burner.'

Li's mind froze. She didn't even dare to speak.

Amber managed a smile. 'But look on the bright side. At least the balloon's filled with helium, not hydrogen.'

The rat-a-tat of bullets stopped.

'Hey,' said Amber, looking around, 'we must be out of range.' She kneeled up carefully again. No more bullets came. She pulled herself to her feet and checked the regulator. 'I'll just close this down.'

Li felt giddy, as though she had been hyperventilating. She looked at Amber standing confidently in the basket and wondered for a moment whether she'd be able to. Then she told herself not to be silly, and forced herself to get up.

'Oh,' said Amber. She was twisting the regulator.

'What?' asked Li.

'Well, I'm trying to turn off the gas and nothing's happening.' Amber's voice was serious. 'And I think this bullet mark might have something to do with it. They hit the burner.'

'What does that mean?'

'It means we're going up and up and we can't stop.'

25
OUT OF CONTROL

'I'll phone Paulo,' said Li. As she put her hand on the phone, she felt it vibrate. Hex's name came up in the window. 'Well, that's good timing.'

'Alex sent me a text,' said Hex. 'He said you were being shot at. Are you OK?'

Amber pulled the sleeve of her fleece over her fingers for protection, and tried again to turn off the gas.

'The regulator's been hit,' said Li. 'The balloon's going up and we can't stop it.'

Hex was silent at the other end.

'Hex? Hello? I suppose it's OK – I mean, it will just carry on up until it runs out, won't it?'

'No,' said Hex, 'it will get hotter and hotter and eventually explode.'

Amber, still trying to turn the gas off, watched Li's face intently. She saw the girl's expression change.

'How long?' whispered Li.

'I don't know. You'll have to jump.'

Li echoed the word back to him faintly. 'Jump?' Surely that wasn't necessary. The burner was roaring, but it sounded like its normal sound. Surely it couldn't be that much of an emergency; not like if a plane was climbing out of control. 'It doesn't feel like it's going up very fast,' she said. Her voice was almost a whisper. 'Are you sure we need to jump?'

'Yes,' said Hex. 'Jump now; you haven't got much time.' He rang off.

Amber gave a great yell as she tried to twist the knob. It wouldn't budge. Exasperated, she let her hands fall to her sides. 'Hex is right. We've climbed at least forty metres in about a minute. Have a look out there if you don't believe me.' She bent down to her parachute, which she had removed so that she could move around the balloon more easily. She manoeuvred her shoulders into the straps and did up the waist belt.

Li felt numb. She didn't know how she was going to do this. She looked over the rim of the basket. The trees were now a long way below. Jump into all that space? She would die.

Amber looked at the altimeter. They were at about five hundred metres, much lower than the usual height for deploying a parachute. They could wait longer before jumping, which would be safer, but how long would they have before the tank blew?

Amber picked up the camcorder, which Li had put in its shockproof carrying case, and clipped it carefully to her own waist belt. Out of the corner of her eye she saw the lights of the buyer's plane as it lifted up through the trees and away into the sky. They were getting away; the evidence in the camcorder was the last hope of catching them. Amber looked down at Li.

Her friend had frozen; she was kneeling in the basket staring over the edge. She should have had her chute back on by now. Didn't she understand how much danger they were in? 'Come on, Li – Hex is right,' Amber said. 'We've got to go now.'

Very stiffly, Li reached for her parachute. She looks horrified by it, thought Amber. 'Here, I'll help you on with it. It's easier.' Li turned like a robot. Her shoulders were rigid as Amber hefted the parachute onto them. 'Li, are you OK?' she said.

The phone flashed up a message. Someone had sent a text. Li opened it.

Amber looked over her shoulder. It was from Paulo. 'UR v brave. U volunteered when scared. Tell Amber. She will help.'

'Tell Amber what?' asked Amber. Her eyes bored into Li's like gimlets.

'I can't jump,' said Li. The words came out as a tumble. 'I nearly had an accident and I'm terrified the chute will break or won't open. And I'm terrified I'll freeze when I'm meant to pull the rip cord.'

Amber shivered; inside she had gone cold as ice. She turned Li round, opened the top of the chute, pulled out a handful of fabric and showed it to Li. 'Li, you know what this is?'

Li nodded. 'The pilot chute. It pulls out the main chute.'

'Right,' said Amber. 'I will hold this while you jump. Then your chute will definitely open.' She glanced nervously at the regulator. The altimeter was still climbing; indeed, it was climbing ever faster as the air pressure dropped. She pushed Li to the edge of the basket. 'I'll take the camcorder. Go now. I don't know how long we've got.'

Li grasped the basket. She put one leg over the wickerwork sill and gripped it hard while she put the other over too. Her limbs felt weak and her insides were like jelly. Every ounce of her body was fighting to stay in the basket.

'On a count of three,' said Amber, 'and I'll see you at the bottom. Three . . . two . . . one . . .'

Li put her hands over her eyes and tipped forwards.

It was like the nightmare. She was falling. In thin air, with nothing to catch her. Pictures flashed through her head like a newsreel played at high speed. A rope breaking loose from a rock face, snaking down through the air past her towards the ground. The rocks waiting below to smash her body. She would scream and scream until medics put her to sleep. Then the pain would go but the agony would remain as she was condemned to a living death. That was what would happen if she didn't get it right; that was the pressure she had never really thought about in her whole life until a few weeks before.

She felt the parachute straps tug her shoulders. The chute was open.

Amber watched Li float away. Her chute had opened safely and her descent slowed.

The balloon continued to soar. Amber lost no time in baling out herself. As soon as her legs pushed away from the hard wicker basket she pulled the chute open. The balloon seemed to shoot up away from her, it was rising so fast.

As Amber's chute opened she had time to look at what was down below: trees, sandy scrubland and a river. Two out of three of those would be bad places to land.

A loud blast hit her head like a blow. She shut her eyes but the flash burned through her eyelids and lit the entire sky. A wave of heat assaulted her, and the flying smithereens of wicker basket lashed her like needles. She tried to shield her face, curling up in the air, but her arms were pulled this way and that by the wind.

It was like being hurled into a rough sea. The shock wave picked her up and pushed her like a giant hand. She had a sudden vision of the air currents turning her upside down, tangling the chute around her so that it no longer carried her but became a useless, crumpled ball of material as she plummeted to the ground. She had to keep her feet pointing downwards – she simply had to.

The canopy of the balloon drifted past her, a huge tangled, twisting mass of orange and silver floating on the turbulent air. Gradually everything steadied. Keeping her position wasn't so hard. After a short while she trusted the parachute to carry her.

Now she could turn her attention to where she was going to land. She had come down quite some distance; the tops of the trees were now a lot closer and the river was below, a slick, glassy surface in the dwindling light.

As her hearing recovered from the blast she heard a loud bellow and a splash. Great. The river was full of hippos. She also remembered there were crocodiles. She felt for the cord to steer the parachute; it operated a flap similar to the one in the top of the balloon. She pulled hard, hoping it would take her away from the river. Would she be in time?

The ground was coming closer. The dark surface of the water was expanding. It must be the Luangwa River; nothing else was that wide. She was now drifting in the direction of one shore. That was a relief. Yes, she was definitely heading for the shore – in fact past it to an escarpment like a small cliff four metres above the water line.

Then she saw the dark shape ambling towards the escarpment. Its head bore a heavy pair of horns like elaborate handlebars. A lone buffalo. And she was going to land right beside it.

The ground was coming up fast – too fast because she had jumped from such a low altitude. She'd have to go with the flow. Amber prepared to roll on impact.

Landing was like hitting a wall. The shock jarred

right through her body and she fell. Something ripped inside her ankle, the same sickening sensation she had felt while out running when she originally injured it. All she was aware of was a white, burning pain in her foot. She tried to stand but the pain erupted up her leg.

Then she spotted the buffalo again, ten metres away. The massive pair of horns curled over the top of his head. He looked straight at her and blew air loudly through his nostrils; he had got her scent. He shook his head, slinging saliva and grass in a wide spray. He grunted and stomped with his right front hoof and snaked his head from side to side like a bull facing a matador.

Then he charged.

Amber forced herself to get to her feet. The wind was blowing towards the river. This bank was much higher than the other: it was her only chance. Adrenaline made her forget the pain. She sprinted to the escarpment. The parachute flared out behind her. The bull thundered behind her. Her boot touched the edge of the cliff and she leaped into the void.

The wind caught her parachute. She glided over the surface of the river and touched down in the mud on the opposite bank.

Li heard the explosion and saw it light up the darkening sky like a giant firework, turning the clouds brilliant orange and yellow. Where was Amber? She had seen a brief silhouette at the moment of the blast. It was burned on her retina like the flash of a camera. For a few seconds Li forgot her own troubles. Was Amber all right?

Then she saw her drifting, away from her and towards the river. She looked OK.

What now? Li had to find somewhere to land. She looked down. She was floating above the trees near the runway. She saw a flash of something moving below – vehicle headlights. It was difficult to work out the shape, but it wasn't the Teak Lodge Jeep or Range Rover. It must be the poachers' vehicle.

She pulled on the cord to change direction. The vehicle below changed direction too, weaving in and out of the trees. She changed direction again. The same thing happened.

The poachers were following her. They were waiting to see where she came down and they were going to ambush her.

She couldn't keep going for much longer. She was losing height all the time. She would have to land very soon. Where would give her the best chance of escape?

She searched the ground. There was only scrubby land and trees – they would have her in no time. Her only chance was a tree. She could at least hide.

She should try to double back a little, too. If she made them go in a circle it would give her time to hide. She would worry about how to get down later.

She spied a group of tall trees. The tops were just metres away from the soles of her boots. She didn't have any choice now. This would have to do.

Her feet grazed the leaves, then sank through the top canopy. Li realized she was going to crash through the branches, pulled her elbows in and hid her face. In moments the tree was crashing and splintering all around her; leaves and branches whipped at her. How far would she fall? She didn't seem to be stopping. Would she go all the way through to the ground?

With a jerk she came to a halt. The harness had caught on something. The blue canopy of the chute floated down like a cloud and turned the twilight into sapphire darkness.

She was dangling nine metres above the ground. She had been wrong to choose a tree. The parachute canopy made her even easier to spot. She had to get moving, now.

She felt over her shoulder for the quick-release catches on the harness. There were none. She undid the waist buckle. When it was released she fell until the shoulder straps caught her. The old panic came back. There was nothing beneath her feet but thin air. No branches to support her weight. The dream came back. The fall. There was the ground. She knew the next thing she had to do was get her shoulders out of the harness, but she couldn't. She would fall.

She heard shouts and the sound of a vehicle reversing. Lights swung through the trees. The poachers were coming. She swung one leg out and caught a branch with it. She hooked the other one over. Now she was suspended between the harness and the branch she had her legs around. She eased one arm out of the harness, then the other. The harness dropped away. Now there was nothing holding her onto the tree but her own raw strength.

She heard the rattle of bullets. The poachers were shooting at the parachute canopy.

She had to get clear of it. She clasped the branch with her hands, pulled herself up to a sitting position and began to climb. The branches were grey and gnarled, as though the trunks of narrower trees had been twisted together. Up and up she went, past all those branches she had broken on her way down. It took seconds for her to get clear of the parachute canopy, but she went on climbing.

Sparks flew off the tree as the poachers peppered the parachute with bullets. How long before they looked across and saw her?

An electronic bleeping pierced through the sound of shooting. Suddenly there was silence.

Li froze. She could just about see them. One of them took something that looked like a mobile phone from his belt. He said a few words in his brutal-sounding dialect while the other poacher gave the parachute a final blast of bullets. Then he sat down and floored the accelerator. The Land Rover turned in a wide arc and left in a cloud of dust.

The moon was taking shape in the dark sky like an image on a developing photograph. Li rested where she was and caught her breath. She was alive.

26
A GOOD NIGHT

Amber saw the headlights coming through the grass. She was sitting on the edge of the river, just far enough away to be out of range of crocodiles or hippos. Her chute was bundled beside her and she couldn't get up.

The headlights gleamed ahead of her. Was it the poachers, come to get her? Could she run from them? The nerves in her ankle were screaming every time she tried to put weight on it. It was worse than last time – possibly even broken. She felt sick, but she would have to force herself to move.

She got onto all fours. She could crawl slowly until she was under cover, leaving the chute where it was.

Then she heard a voice. 'This is where it says she is. But I can't see anything.' It was Alex's peculiar flattened accent.

'Alex?' called Amber. She kneeled up.

Alex was standing up in the Jeep. He saw Amber rise from the reeds by the river bed.

Hex was behind him, Paulo at the wheel. Hex was holding the elephant-tracing device. 'Told you she'd be here,' he said.

'How did you find me?' Amber's face relaxed in a wide, relieved smile. Her eyes gleamed in the headlights.

Paulo answered: 'While you were sleeping, Hex tranquillized you and Li and put tags in you.'

The gleam in Amber's eyes changed to a different sort of look; a steely glint.

It was enough to make Hex's blood run cold. 'No I didn't,' he said quickly. 'I put tags in your parachutes. Just in case.'

'Did you get the shots of the poachers?' said Alex.

Amber's eyes were round and horrified. 'Oh my God, I left the camcorder in the balloon.'

The three boys all chorused, 'What?!'

Amber grinned at them. 'No, it's here.' She held up the camcorder, safe and sound. 'But one of you will have to come and carry me.'

Amber aboard, Paulo drove slowly off, following Hex's directions. 'This,' said Hex, looking at the bleeping detector, 'should be Li.'

Paulo braked and looked around. 'Where?' The Jeep's headlights picked out the base of a strangler fig tree.

Alex squinted into the darkness. There was a shape, greyish looking, clinging to the side of the tree. 'There . . . I think.' He got out a torch and flashed the beam over it. It showed up royal blue. 'That looks like a parachute.'

Paulo looked at the tree. If Li was up there, she'd need help getting down. Should he try to conceal it from the others? And how would they get her down anyway? He didn't think he could get up something like that.

From the tree came a crackle as branches

snapped and twigs broke. A shape was coming down through the branches – possibly a baboon.

But it wasn't. A slim, female shape dropped confidently out of the foliage and landed like a trapeze artist.

'What took you so long?' Li grinned.

Paulo, Alex and Hex got out to help her pull the parachute out of the tree. They got the canopy down but the harness was caught about two metres up. 'Li,' said Alex, 'you'll have to go back up for it.'

Li put her hand on the tree, ready to climb up again. Then she felt a prickle at the back of her neck, as though someone was standing right behind her. She turned and found Paulo looking at her, his face a question. Her upturned eyes met his for a moment in the light from the headlamps, reassuring him.

He understood, and smiled. 'I told you you'd work it out,' he said quietly.

'I did,' she agreed in a whisper, 'but I was wrong. I was struggling to do it on my own. I should have known when to accept help; that's part of teamwork. You kept trying to help me and I wouldn't let you. Instead I struggled on my own and wouldn't let anyone in. In the end, you did save me; you and Amber. If you hadn't made me tell her, I wouldn't be here now.'

'Stop smooching, you two,' called Alex. 'We've got to get this chute down.'

Li flashed Paulo a smile, then turned, grasped some branches and levered herself up. She caught the harness and gave it a hard tug. It came down in a shower of branches and Li jumped nimbly back down.

'I'm afraid it's full of holes,' she said. 'The poachers took pot shots at me. Then they got a call on their bleeper thing and decided they'd shot me enough.' Her tone changed.

'That'll be their detector. They must be out getting another elephant,' said Hex.

'I think they'll find it's something else . . .' said Alex.

The poacher with the scarred cheek drove the Land Rover. His partner with the hyena tooth had the detector. He watched its winking light greedily.

'We just got paid and already there's more ivory

out there, calling to us,' said Hyena-tooth. 'It's going to be a good night. Stop here.'

Scarface braked and cut the engine. He reached over the seat for his gun. With the heel of his hand he slammed another magazine in.

The poachers climbed out. Hyena-tooth consulted his tracer again and nodded in the direction it indicated. Scarface checked which way the wind was blowing. Then the two poachers went forwards cautiously. Until they fired their shots they would work in silence. The elephants were so easily startled away.

Scarface stopped and listened. Hyena-tooth, attuned to his movements, did the same; then his companion walked on.

Scarface stopped again. The moon was up so he could see quite well, but he wasn't quite sure what he was looking at. It seemed to be a lion, a big shape with a strong musky smell. His tail twitched like a long, lazy skipping rope.

Scarface glanced at Hyena-tooth. The other poacher was looking at the detector. 'It must have scared away the elephant.' He raised his gun.

Suddenly both poachers were knocked to the ground as powerful feline bodies cannoned into them. Then it started: a frenzy of roaring as the lions went in for the kill. Two screams rang out briefly but the howls drowned them and echoed across the night sky.

Driving back, Alpha Force heard the screams. Paulo slowed; when the drone of the engine faded the five heard the unmistakable sounds of lions squabbling over a kill. That lasted just moments and gave way to loud purring, eerie and savage.

Alpha Force listened, awestruck.

Alex was the first to speak. His voice was grim. 'That's the first time the mice went looking for the cats.'

27
A NEW BEGINNING

Paulo turned the Jeep off the road and into the bush.

'Mind the baboons,' laughed Li, as a family of the creatures skittered away from the wheels.

It was the morning after the poachers' rendezvous on the airstrip. Alpha Force had been to the hospital, where Amber's ankle was X-rayed and strapped up. Nothing was broken, but the ligaments were ripped and needed complete rest. While Amber was being treated, Joe had been delighted to find the others in the waiting room. He was on his way back from dropping the evidence off at the police station and had good news – Tessa was sitting up in bed and was ready to have visitors.

Now Alpha Force were in the Jeep, on one last mission in the park. Paulo drove; Alex sat beside him with the detector. Hex was in the back with Amber and Li, and the camcorder. They were going to prepare a surprise for Tessa when she got home.

'What a relief to see her looking so well,' said Amber.

'Wasn't it weird, though,' said Hex. 'After what Patrick told us I kept looking at the bed to see if she still had both legs.'

Amber squealed and her hands flew up to her mouth. 'I did too. And she saw me staring – it was so embarrassing.'

'I don't think she'd been told she nearly lost her leg, do you?' said Paulo.

'No,' agreed Amber. 'And I didn't want to be the one to tell her.'

'Joe did the right thing telling her about Moya, though,' said Li. 'Better she hears now than coming back and discovering an empty pen.'

Alex, in the front seat, was looking at the detector. 'I think they're close. Just bear left a bit, Paulo.'

Amber was looking over his shoulder, trying to get a view of the detector. 'It's definitely Thunderbird and the others, is it? Tessa will know if we get the wrong elephants.'

Hex, beside her, gave her a withering look. '*We* may not know one pachyderm from another, but that little box does.'

'And we can definitely get this printed and so on before she gets back?' said Li.

Hex patted his waist belt. 'I've got the palmtop right here. We shoot some footage, choose some good stills, e-mail them to the shop I found, and they'll print them out as posters. Then Joe picks them up on his way back from the police and we put them up in her room. Hey presto – Brains, Penelope and Thunderbird on her wall, welcoming her home in person.'

Paulo turned round briefly. 'Hey, I could get on Thunderbird for one of the pictures,' he said proudly. 'That would give Tessa a surprise.'

'Actually,' Amber whispered to Li, 'Tessa told me she used to ride Thunderbird when she was little.'

Li's eyes widened. She glanced at Paulo, who was concentrating on steering around some marula trees. 'You're kidding!' she hissed. 'The fraud!'

'I didn't have the heart to tell him,' said Amber. 'He's been so proud of himself. And she had a Spanish ranger to help her, so that's why Thunderbird took to Paulo.'

Li put her hand over her mouth, but she couldn't stop the giggles that erupted inside her like a geyser.

Hex looked at them, his expression begging to be told.

'Girl thing,' said Amber through clenched teeth. 'I'll tell you later.'

'If Thunderbird was Tessa's childhood playmate, it's a good thing we kept her out of that minefield,' Li whispered to Amber. 'But that elephant certainly knows how to get into trouble.'

Alex was still monitoring the detector. 'They're just here,' he said.

'Is it all three of them?' said Paulo.

'Looks like it,' said Alex. 'Get ready with the camera, Hex.'

'I'll put it on zoom so we don't have to go too close,' said Hex.

Paulo slowed the Jeep and let it crawl as it came round the tree. In the distance, the three craggy grey shapes were feeding from an acacia tree. The trunks went up like periscopes, sniffed the air and then relaxed again. The Jeep and its occupants had been registered, and accepted as friendly.

Hex put the camcorder to his eye and focused.

'Do you think we can go closer?' said Paulo.

'I think they might not want us to right now,' said Hex, his eye to the viewfinder. He pressed pause and handed the camcorder to Amber.

Amber lifted it to her eye. When she saw what Hex had been looking at, she gasped. She was about to blurt out what she was seeing, but then she bit her tongue. It would be more fun if her friends saw for themselves. She lowered the camera without saying anything, and passed it to Li.

Li, intrigued, looked through the viewfinder. A big smile broke out on her face.

'What is it?' said Alex. But Li put her fingers to her lips in a shushing movement and simply handed the camera to him.

Alex looked at the elephants. He saw what the others had seen. He could feel Paulo's eyes burning into him with curiosity, waiting for an explanation. Alex decided to play it very, very cool. He nodded to himself sagely and handed the camcorder to Paulo.

When Paulo looked through the viewfinder he saw: a tiny, wrinkled grey shape standing in front of Thunderbird. The big elephant was caressing it with her trunk, her ears paddling gently back and forth in an expression of contentment. Penelope and Brains were busy pulling down branches of acacia and piling them up for a feast.

A big grin spread across Paulo's face. 'Wow,' he said. 'Thunderbird's had a calf.'

'All this time she was pregnant,' said Li. 'Why didn't it show?'

'Just look at all that baggy skin she's got,' said Alex. 'We had no way of knowing. Even the rangers didn't know.'

Paulo was filming. The grin on his face was enormous. 'The calf's getting up to suckle. It looks strong and healthy. Just wait until Tessa sees this.'

EPILOGUE

The first-class lounge of Lusaka airport was quiet. Lam Lau-Ke always relished the moment he walked through its doors. The hurly burly of flight calls and bored passengers killing time, the heady fug of fast food all disappeared. Instead there was a gentle clinking as clean crystal glasses were placed on the bar, the smell of leather furniture and the subtle hint of expensive aftershave. He looked at his watch: an hour until his dawn flight to Hong Kong. There was time for a refreshing drink.

He carried a sturdy flight bag; it was Louis Vuitton

– nothing else would take the weight of the ivory time after time. He always carried it with him as hand baggage, never trusted it to the hold. It took him over the baggage allowance, but that could always be sorted out by paying a fee here and there. The airport staff were used to rich international travellers who preferred to keep their valuable items closely guarded.

The pilot had flown him to Lusaka from the pick-up in the jungle. Again there was nothing unusual about this: small chartered planes came in from game parks all over the country as a matter of routine. As usual, he'd gone by a circuitous route so that it wasn't obvious which park he had come from; the journey had taken five hours instead of two. You could never be too careful.

The handover this time hadn't gone as smoothly as he'd liked, but Lam Lau-Ke accepted that you had a rough ride once in a while. That was the nature of the business. The people in the balloon were probably just tourists from one of the lodges and didn't know what they were seeing. That was why the tusks were cut up into small pieces; so tourists wouldn't know what they were.

He went to the bar and ordered a gin and tonic. He felt he had definitely earned it. He barely noticed the two figures who came in through the door. They wore the local police uniform. They must have wandered in by mistake. He turned his attention to the view of the taxiing area outside. Planes glided past on their way to the runway, the livery painted on their tails giving a hint of far-flung destinations – Singapore Airlines, Qantas, Emirates. Soon he would be sitting in first class on board a Cathay Pacific bound for Chek Lap Kok in Hong Kong.

The barman put his drink on the mahogany counter. Its sparkling depths looked long, cool and refreshing. His hand went to the glass.

'Mr Lam?' said a voice behind him.

Annoyed, he looked round. It was the two policemen. They both carried sub-machine guns.

'Would you come with us, please,' said one of them. 'We have a warrant for your arrest.'

CHRIS RYAN'S TOP SAS TIPS ON DEALING WITH WILD ANIMALS

Africa is teeming with dangerous animals. They may appear harmless and passive, but they can attack with blinding speed. Your most important weapon is *knowledge*. If you are lucky enough to be travelling or on safari in Africa, do take the time to learn about the animals you might meet there before you set out, and pay attention to anything the local guides tell you. Li knows a lot about different animals, but she and the rest of Alpha Force still find they have a lot to learn during their stay. In a tricky situation, knowing how an animal thinks could save your life!

SOME BASIC FACTS ABOUT WILD ANIMALS

- Animals don't attack because they want to eat you. They attack because they think you've *threatened* them – usually by getting too close. People *have* been killed by lions – in one incident simply because they drove right up to the lions and then got out to take a close-up photo. This doesn't means that you can't still observe dangerous animals – just remember to keep at a safe distance. Even lions will avoid you if you don't get too close.

- Many people say that wild animals are more afraid of us than we are of them. This is probably true, but rather misleading. When wild animals are afraid, they don't do what a human does and run away. Instead, they get very, very bad tempered – and it's generally not a good idea to encounter a bad-tempered wild animal on its home territory!

- Wild animals will defend the territory around them: it is where they find their food and rear their family, and if you encroach upon it they think that you want to hurt them or their young, or steal their food or their mate.

- When you approach big game – even at a very safe distance – be cautious and quiet: no loud noises and no sudden movements. And if they are nursing their young, or eating, or mating, they should be given an even wider berth.

- Always avoid approaching animals that look as though they might be wounded or ill. They will be more likely to panic because they can't run away. And beware of any animal that has become separated from its herd – it may feel anxious without the support of its companions. In Africa you could also come across an animal that's been tranquillized, perhaps for medical treatment or for tagging. Although it may look dopey it could wake up in an instant with a big fright. So steer well clear.

- Never, ever go near any young animal; its parents will be close by. If you get between a young animal and its parents, you could be in big trouble. A baby animal might look soft and cuddly, but its parent certainly won't be, so avoid it!

- Don't try to feed animals, or leave food for them.

If you do, eventually they will lose their fear of humans. Then they can become a nuisance and a danger, entering villages and campsites to steal food. If this happens, the authorities may have to destroy them so you aren't doing them any favours in the long run. If you're camping in an area near to where wild animals roam, don't leave food lying about – it will tempt them in. Dispose of litter carefully, especially if it's been in contact with food.

● Finally, never corner or tease a wild animal. You might think that's common sense, but safari organizers have to point this out to tourists time and time again.

WHAT KIND OF ANIMALS MIGHT YOU ENCOUNTER IN AFRICA?

There are two kinds of animals – *predators*, which hunt their food and are carnivorous (this means they could eat *you*); and *herbivores* – animals that eat grasses and vegetation. Even though herbivores don't want to eat you, it doesn't necessarily mean they are safe to be around. Just remember what that herbivorous elephant did to the poacher who upset it!

PREDATORS

Here are some of the more common predators you could see in Africa:

Lions

The big cats just want easy lives and don't necessarily see you as food. But never take this for granted; you never know if the cat you've met is desperately hungry, or ill and afraid. Lions can smell blood from miles away and will home in on an injured animal.

If you find yourself confronting a big cat, don't run. That's the worst thing you can do, as you'll trigger its kill response. Shout and wave your arms, trying to make yourself look as big as possible. A predator needs to remain fit in order to survive, so if you look as though you might injure it, it may let you go. Although every instinct in your body might be telling you to run away, you have to do exactly the opposite and stand your ground.

I've heard stories from safari guides who had experienced being charged by a lion. As the lion got closer and closer, they continued to shout and scream, and it was only at the last minute that it roared and turned away. Needless to say, it was very frightening.

Be especially careful around predators in the early morning. Most of their hunting is done at night, so you'll be likely to come across feeding animals at dawn. If you see vultures circling in the sky, move away because you may be near to lions feeding on a kill. At night, if you hear lions roaring, there has probably been a kill nearby. Move away, because male lions will be coming in to eat and you might cross their path.

Crocodiles

Crocs are also vicious predators. They skulk close to the banks of rivers, ready to grab likely prey, or fight off threats to their territory. They'll grab any animal, humans included. By the time they pounce, it's usually too late – although people have escaped crocodile attacks by thumping them hard on the soft part of the nose.

If you're walking or camping near to croc-infested waters, keep a good distance away from the bank – at least ten metres. If you're in a boat, don't dangle your arms and legs over the side or you might provoke an attack.

HERBIVORES

Hippos

Harmless herbivores? No. In Africa more people are killed by the hippopotamus than by any other animal. They look cuddly, clumsy and harmless, but they are very aggressive and territorial and they can run 100 metres in nine seconds – so if they chase you, they will catch you.

Hippos can move just as fast in water as they can on land and will attack boats – although not if they have engines. When I was in the regiment we were paddling an inflatable boat up a river at night with the engine off so that we could move silently. It was pitch black and suddenly this great mouth loomed out of the water and bit the end off the boat. Because it was an inflatable it went bang, which scared the hippo off; otherwise it would have tipped us out and gored us with its tusks.

Hippos are also incredibly strong. In Botswana, when we were filming *Hunting Chris Ryan*, I found a six-metre crocodile that had been bitten in two by a hippo.

On land, they're just as bad-tempered. If you get between a hippo and the water's edge, it will feel threatened: it will panic and you'll be trampled. Be even more careful to avoid hippos during the dry season, as the waterways shrink – and it's also the time when they're looking out for mates.

Elephants

Although man and elephant can work together – elephants are often used to carry people on their backs and Alpha Force begin to make friends with Moya and the other elephants in the reserve – elephants can be dangerous. One reason is because their eyesight is bad. Always stay upwind of them because if they smell or hear you they'll panic and attack. When I was in the regiment I lost two mates when elephants smelled us in our laying-up point and charged. They trampled everything that was in their way; nothing stopped them.

Oddly enough, it's the same tactic the army use when caught in an ambush – turn and attack with maximum aggression.

Buffalo

If you find buffalo tracks or droppings, steer clear. If you get close enough to see them, back away immediately. Buffalo are very dangerous and cunning, even in herds. The whole herd is controlled by a couple of massive bulls – a lead scout and a tail-end charlie. If they feel threatened they can turn the entire mass of animals onto you – even at a flat-out gallop. And if you ever come across a buffalo on its own, move away fast as it will charge. They're so strong that they can gore a lion to death with a single toss of their horns.

Harmless-looking?

It's not just the big animals you have to worry about. Even the harmless-looking antelopes could give you a nasty injury. Thompson's gazelle, which is less than a metre high and looks like Bambi, has small,

dagger-like horns that it uses in battles over territory – and it will not hesitate to battle with you if
you wander into its patch.

And man, of course

It's often said that the biggest danger to the animals
in Africa is *man*. Man can also be the biggest threat
to you, too: another real hazard in Africa is
poachers. They all carry weapons and they shoot
to kill. Avoid them at all costs.

SNAKES

In addition to the large animals that live in Africa,
there are a lot of smaller creatures to be careful of
– insects, spiders and, especially, snakes.

Top tips for dealing with snakes!

- Snakes are usually as keen to avoid you as you
  are to avoid them. When I was filming in
  Botswana, a snake-handler gave us a demonstra-
  tion: even the most aggressive ones would slither
  harmlessly over your foot if you just stood
  quietly. Often you don't even realize a snake is

there until you hear it move away. The key is not to disturb them. If you see a snake, the best thing to do is simply stand still and let it go on its way, then proceed as normal.

- It's a good idea to wear sturdy boots, thick socks and long trousers if you're in an area where snakes are found. Long sleeves are a good idea too and they'll also protect you from insect bites – some insects, such as mosquitoes, can carry nasty diseases.

- If you're about to step into shade, look around carefully, or if it's dark, shine a torch on the ground. If you step over a log, look carefully at the other side before you put your feet down.

- If you're searching the ground around fallen trees, stones or thick grass, don't do it with your hands – use a long pole or branch.

- Never try to pick up a snake or gather all your friends to show them what you've found. When I was in Honduras making *Hunting Chris Ryan*, I called the crew over to look at an extremely venomous Fer de Lance snake I'd found in the bathroom. Big mistake. When all those people gathered around it, it attacked blindingly fast. It moved *five metres* in the blink of an eye. Fortunately the guide came to our rescue, but he wouldn't have had to if I'd left it alone.

- Be especially careful in the early morning. Snakes will be sluggish then because the temperature is cooler, and if you take them by surprise they won't be able to move away as quickly, so they might attack. This is why most snake attacks happen – or because someone prodded one.

- Some snakes spit venom. If it gets in open cuts or in your eyes you must wash it out thoroughly and immediately. Use any liquid that comes to hand – even urine.

- If you need to kill a snake, break its back by whacking it with a long, heavy stick, as close as possible to the head. Make sure you hit it really hard – a wounded snake is very dangerous.

You may also come across poisonous scorpions and spiders in Africa. If you are camping, they may find their way into your boots – so shake them out before you put them on in the morning!

FIRST AID

All members of the SAS are trained in field first aid and carry a medical kit so that we can deal with injuries on operations. First-aid skills are always valuable and any expedition into a situation of potential danger should include at least one person with some medical skills. Everyone, however, should know how to deal with basic injuries, so why not try and take a few classes locally so that you can offer basic skills yourself?

Bites

Although if you're careful the chances of being bitten by an animal are small, it's as well to know what to do if it does happen. All bites, even from animals that do not carry venom, can cause nasty infections from bacteria in the animal's mouth, and cats, canines and apes may carry rabies and tetanus.

If someone is bitten, get them to hospital immediately – even minor-looking bites can be very serious; if that isn't possible, you should give the appropriate first aid, keep the victim calm and aim to get them further medical help as soon as possible.

Wash the wound with soap and water to remove any dirt and saliva. Check that they are breathing OK and be ready to give mouth-to-mouth resuscitation. Do not give them anything containing alcohol or tobacco to help them get over the shock, but be prepared to deal with symptoms of shock (see below).

If you have been bitten by a snake, scorpion or spider, it is very important to stay calm: any venom in the bloodstream will travel round faster if the victim panics. Don't try to suck the wound to get the venom out – you may poison yourself, and in any case, some may have already entered the victim's bloodstream. Never try to cut out venom either; you'll definitely drive it further into the system. And if you touch the area yourself, be very careful not to transfer the venom; don't touch your own eyes, mouth or anywhere else without washing your hands thoroughly.

Many snakebites (and bites from spiders and some insects) are treated with specific antivenoms; the most common of these will almost certainly be kept at local medical centres – often in safari camps themselves for emergency use. For example, when Patrick finds the injured poacher by the roadside, he calls the medical services and is instructed to give the man an adrenaline injection from supplies kept at the camp.

It is always useful if you can identify the snake or insect that has injected the venom. If possible – and without risk to yourself – kill the snake; if you can't, try to remember the identifying features as clearly as possible: this information could save a life as doctors can administer the correct antivenom promptly. If washing the venom out, try to keep a sample on the cloth you used, as doctors may also be able to analyse any venom to identify what antidote to give.

Whatever the bite was caused by, keep the wound covered, but check for redness, heat and swelling – this indicates infection. If infection occurs, keep the wound uncovered and clean with soap.

Any signs of poisoning will usually appear within two hours. Signs to watch for include bleeding from the nose or other orifices, blood in the urine, breathing difficulty, paralysis, twitching and numbness.

Wounds

Major wounds that are bleeding heavily will clearly need medical attention as soon as possible. An average person has just over six litres of blood circulating in their body. If you lose about half a litre, you feel a bit faint (this is why blood donors have to lie down for a short time after donating blood), but losing as much as a litre and a half could cause collapse; more than this could lead to death. Bleeding can often be stopped by simply applying pressure over the point of blood loss. Use the cleanest material available, press over the wound and keep the pressure on for five to ten minutes before bandaging the dressing in place.

If the bleeding is arterial – pumping out at the same rate as the victim's pulse – you may need to apply a tourniquet as Alpha Force do to Tessa's leg. A tourniquet should only ever be applied to a limb – on the upper arm, just below the armpit, or around the top part of a thigh. However, it is very important that you know what you are doing with a tourniquet: the pressure must be released at regular intervals if the limb is to be saved. This is an instance where there is no substitute for training.

Shock

Shock can kill. The initial shock to the system can cause the blood pressure to drop rapidly, and the victim may look in a state of collapse, with cold, sweaty skin, a feeble but rapid pulse and shakiness. Delayed shock can occur after an injury too. The most important thing to remember is to appear calm and in control of the situation – just holding someone's hand can help a great deal and rest will be essential. Loosen any tight clothing and, if possible, let the person lie down flat with their legs raised slightly.

BE SAFE!

Chris Ryan

Random House Children's Books and Chris Ryan would like to make it clear that this advice is given for use in a serious situation only, where your life could be at risk. We cannot accept any liability for inappropriate usage in normal conditions.

About the Author

Chris Ryan joined the SAS in 1984 and has been involved in numerous operations with the regiment. During the Gulf War, he was the only member of an eight-man team to escape from Iraq, three colleagues being killed and four captured. It was the longest escape and evasion in the history of the SAS. For this he was awarded the Military Medal. He wrote about his remarkable escape in the adult bestseller *The One That Got Away* (1995), which was also adapted for screen.

He left the SAS in 1994 and is now the author of a number of bestselling thrillers for adults. His work in security takes him around the world and he has also appeared in a number of television series, most recently *Hunting Chris Ryan*, in which his escape and evasion skills were demonstrated to the max. The *Alpha Force* titles are his first books for young readers.

If you enjoyed this book, you might like to read
the first Alpha Force adventure:

ALPHA FORCE

Mission: Survival

SURVIVAL

Alex, Li, Paulo, Hex and Amber are five teenagers on
board a sailing ship crewed by young people from all
over the world. Together they are marooned on a desert
island. And together they must face the ultimate test –
survival! Battling against unbelievable dangers – from
killer komodo dragons to sharks and modern-day pirates
– the five must combine all their knowledge and skills if
they are to stay alive.

The team – Alpha Force – is born . . .

ISBN 0 099 43924 7

If you enjoyed this book look out for others in the series:

ALPHA FORCE

Target: Child-Slavers

DESERT PURSUIT

Alpha Force are a unique group of five individuals, each with special skills, each ready to go anywhere in the world to help others in need. Undercover, they head for the Sahara Desert, resolved to gather evidence of young landmine victims. But they are catapulted into a desperate race across the desert when they discover a terrible evil – a gang of child-slavers operating in the area.

The team is in pursuit . . .

ISBN 0 099 43926 3

If you enjoyed this book look out for others in the series:

ALPHA FORCE

Target: Toxic Waste

HOSTAGE

Alpha Force are five teenagers who have formed a highly-skilled squad to help in the international fight against evil. Flying to Northern Canada to investigate reports of illegal dumping of toxic waste, the team must dive into an icy river, cross the harsh landscape on snowmobiles and mobilize their caving skills to complete their mission. But they need all their courage and determination when they come face-to-face with a man who is ready to kill – or take a hostage – to stop them.

The team face their toughest challenge yet . . .

ISBN 0 099 43927 1

If you enjoyed this book look out for others in the series:

ALPHA FORCE

Target: Terrorist Hostage Taker

RED CENTRE

The five members of Alpha Force train hard and are
prepared to go anywhere in the world to combat injustice.
Recruited to help on a survival show in Australia, they
are suddenly thrust into a terrifying ordeal when a hunted
terrorist takes desperate measures to escape capture.
Alongside the Australian SAS, Alpha Force must act
quickly to save lives – even if it means facing the
terrifying heat of an out-of-control bushfire . . .

ISBN 0 099 46424 1